I0617921

The New York Literary Society

New York

Three Gymnopédies

for literature

by

Iimani David

**The New York
Literary Society**

New York   2019

Copyright © 2019 by Iimani David

All rights reserved. Published in the United States by
The New York Literary Society, Ltd.,
New York

No part of this book may be reproduced, stored in a retrieval system, or transmitted by any means without the written permission of the author.

Library of Congress Control Number:
David, Iimani, 1969 –
Three Gymnopédies for Literature / Iimani David
ISBN 978-1-7336412-0-3 Paperback

www.nylsCARES.org

Printed in the United States of America

Loneliness is a negating anti-person. As real in the universe as dark matter and equally unseeable.

Again, for my daughter

Jasmine-Jolie

Three Gymnopédies

for literature

by

Iimani David

Contents

To the reader:

    In 1888, French composer, Erik Satie, wrote three pieces for solo piano and called them *Trois Gymnopédies*. According to Satie, each solo piece was written to examine a common theme, but from a different perspective.

    The stories you will read on the following pages have been written with similar intent. They have in their fabric loneliness, loss and transformation, woven as interlocking themes which are examined in each story from a different perspective. I have chosen to call this literary offering *Three Gymnopédies for Literature*, in honor of Satie's composition, which has given me many years of joy and has aided me during countless hours of reflection.

— Iimani David

Three Gymnopédies

for literature

• π •

Pathétique

It happened again late last night. It was 2:17 a.m., precisely. The rumbling sounds came in quick succession and were heavy and protracted. This time, though, there was scratching. Scratching and clawing. Scratching and clawing that sent chills through my body as the sound echoed within the room. A slow, deep, long clawing that I could not blot out. It and the rumbling were coming from the same place. They were coming from underneath my bed.

I sat up in bed after a long look at the clock on the night table. I had some difficulty focusing my mind, but finally the time registered and I knew I would remember it. I knew, somehow, that it would be important later. I sat up, reached over, and palmed the pack of Slims my girlfriend left beside the clock; tapped out a fag, and lit it. I lit it with the gold and jadestone lighter she gave me for my birthday the prior year, took a long drag, and rested my head back against the headboard. I could feel the vibrations of the clawing shimmy through the frame of the bed. There was something or someone very awful underneath my bed. I knew it. I could feel it.

Buzzing bee, busying by. No need to fear, my dear. No need to cry. Pretty, pretty flowers are all that I

find. No need to fear what's in my mind.

I didn't move for quite some time except for the push and pull of the fag in my left hand to and from my lips. I twiddled the lighter in my right—in my right, because *right* is righteous: I had lost my mobile phone. Notwithstanding the strands of moonlight that snaked their way through the naked April trees outside my window, my room seemed to me: dark. The floor: dark. The wall opposite, though reflecting *this* moon's bluish halo, in its own way seemed: dark. My mind's shadows thickened. I could feel the vibrations. The clawing. The vibrations of the clawing. They were long and slow. Long, slow, and determined.

I first heard the rumbling two nights ago. It was shortly after 2 a.m., Thursday, when it began, though I can't say with certainty the specific time. I had been out with a few friends and had drunk heavily that night. When I returned to my flat, I remember kicking off my shoes at the foot of the bed and allowing myself to fall, like a stone, face down onto the mattress, with arms stretched wide. I was fully clothed except for a denim jacket I had removed at the foyer door and thrown over the arm of a leather chair that resided near there.

Vertigo beset me as I lay on the bed with closed eyes. A light perspiration sheathed my body in the darkness. I didn't feel like moving. Through the blackness the soft electronic ring of my cordless phone beckoned to me from the night table, and I knew it was my girlfriend. I didn't answer it. I did not answer the telephone. *Dizziness*. Dizziness and a nauseated ache in my stomach precluded me. My body was becoming more heavily wet with perspiration. I felt heavy. I felt as though I weighed a thousand pounds.

The phone continued its ringing. *Tiari*. My head felt heavy and my hearing seemed as though in a drum; as though I was lying face down at the bottom of a deep pool filled with hot water. It distorted the phone's ring, giving it a muddled, muffled sound. Even the silence between the rings was bent and distorted. Somewhere, off in the distance, I could hear a child crying.

I felt a rumbling then. I felt it and I heard it. It felt as though it was coming from the center of my chest and its reverberation was faint. I ignored it. Then, I felt the strange sensation of something outlining my body from under my mattress. I was heavily wet now with perspiration. *Dizziness*. I was face down. Somewhere, there was a phone ringing. It was a muffled, muddled ring. It continued with no one to answer it. The sensation went outward from the faint rumbling in my chest to my right armpit and began outlining my body. It traveled down my right side, over my hip, and continued down my leg in a slow, smooth glide. Something on the other side of my mattress was exploring me. Something was feeling and tracing the contour of my body in an attempt to ascertain who, or what, I was. It outlined my right foot and came slowly up the inside of my right leg. I felt heavy. I felt heavy and my head was hot. It passed my right knee. A thousand pounds—I felt as though I weighed a thousand pounds. It passed my knee and continued its slow, deliberate glide up my inner thigh. It dawned on me. Something was happening to me. Something was happening to me, again. I began to cry. I became afraid.

Buzzing bee, busying by. No need to fear, my dear. No need to cry. Pretty, pretty flowers...

It traveled my inner thigh and reached my groin. The pain was excruciating. Moving as entities apart from me, my palms flexed from agony and grabbed desperately at the sheets. My eyelids tensed. In an involuntary action, my lips warped themselves. The pain was of a deep, baritonal variety that fractured my essence and caused my already nauseated stomach to convulse. I couldn't get up. Not that I tried, because I did not. I knew from past experiences that trying to wake would have been futile.

The sensation turned and continued its outline down the inside of my left leg, passed my knee, and approached my foot. The throbbing in my groin subsided, but persisted. My face was wet with perspiration and tears. Somewhere, off in the distance, I could hear the muddled, muffled sound of a telephone, but still, no one would answer it. Somewhere, off in the distance, I could hear a child weeping.

"Don't go."

I felt heavy. The muddled sound of the ringing, coupled with the sobbing and sniffling of the child, made me ill again—in my stomach. The sensation traveled up the left side of my body. Something under my mattress was probing me. I continued to cry.

Buzzing bee, busying by. No need to fear...

It traveled up to my left armpit but did not outline my arm. It, instead, veered right and returned to the center of my chest, where it had started. It rumbled there a moment, then resumed its slow, calculating movement toward my throat—cutting my air as it passed over my trachea. *Behind* my face a singeing heat arose as the probing sensation

reached it, causing a wild beating to ensue beneath my eyes
as I lay face down at the bottom of the pool: the bottom
of a deep pool filled with hot water. A thousand pounds
of pressure was cracking the walls of my skull. My skull.
My skull was cracking. I sensed the heat of the water as it
crashed through the walls of my skull. I opened my mouth
to scream. My mouth opened. Then, everything became
dark.

I awoke later that morning with the left side of my
face lying half buried in vomit. The smell of it made my
stomach retch. Slowly lifting my head and bringing in my
arms, I listlessly began the process of raising my upper
body from the mattress. There was dampness at my waist;
an odd dampness that could only mean that I'd urinated
on myself. I had urinated myself and slept in it; vomited on
myself and slept in that as well.

Standing at the foot of the bed, I pressed my palms
against my face, inhaling deeply as I thought. It was clear
that I couldn't tell Tiari what had occurred. Everything
had to appear normal. I peeled off my clothes, allowing
each item to drop where I stood. I then initiated a slow
segue into the master bathroom to wash up. The bathroom
mirror was unforgiving in its assessment, reflecting the
pathetic definition of a human being that I was. I thought
about its unyielding criticism and remembered a time
when I was proud of my reflection: standing six foot
one with broad shoulders and an athletic build; always
satisfactorily well endowed each time I looked. At twenty-
five years of age, though, the youthful appearance stood
irreconcilable with the "old soul" that resided within.

I gazed a moment longer at *the disappointment* and
noticed a discoloration on its chest. It was slight, occupying
only a small area between the pectoral muscles. Touching

its counterpart brought no discomfort. After wetting my index finger at the tap, I rubbed the discolored area, but nothing changed, as I had hoped it would. Whatever it was, it wasn't a stain of any kind. It was dark, ominously bruise-*like*, and new. It was certainly new. Leaving it, I doused my face with cold water, exited the bathroom, and began the task of making my bed a proper place; determining to discard everything except the sheets so as not to arouse too much suspicion in Tiari by their absence.

Without ceremony or fear, I dropped to my knees and peered underneath the bed, reasonably sure from past experiences that I wouldn't find anything there. The *dark* side was bleak and dusty, but nothing seemed unusual. Standing up, I moved to the side of the bed in preparation to lift the mattress, hoping to drag it to the front door of the flat, thereby making it easier for the building's porter to remove. Slipping my fingers between the mattress and the bed's frame, I raised the thing and tilted it upwards until it was perpendicular to the floor and might stand on its own.

What I saw alarmed me. As the mattress began its slow downward pivot, I moved quickly to re-collect my clothing; snatching items from the floor as the sound of the mattress crashing back down upon on its frame reached me. I rushed toward the front door, dressing in tandem, grabbed my denim jacket from the chair, and hurried into the presumed safety of the sunlit world.

*   *   *

I felt sick. I felt an awful sickness. In my stomach there was a dull heaviness; an inexplicable weight deep inside that filled me with foreboding. It made my body hot. My body was hot.

My head, too, was sick. Sick from exhaustion. Sick from not eating. Sick from worry. Every now and again, when I would try to focus my eyes, there would come an acute pain in my temples. So, I stopped trying to focus my eyes and instead closed them and hung my head. I closed my eyes, leaned forward, rested my forearms on my knees, and registered the taxi's motion as it crossed the bridge and made its way to the on ramp of the FDR Drive. I wasn't well. Something inside me wasn't well. I could feel it. I didn't know what it was. I didn't know what was happening to me. I desperately needed peace. I needed there to be quiet so I could focus my mind and settle my head. An incessant rattling from the boot of the car, however—though it had no apparent effect on the driver—knotted my nerves. I sat leaned forward, feeling the warmth of the mobile phone in my right hand. It was warm and wet with perspiration. Replaying the voicemail in my head only heightened the alarm in Tiari's voice. The panic behind her words still reverberated within me.

The stinging in my groin continued. The discolored area on my chest, though it didn't sting, caused me concern. I did all I could to suppress the persistent vulgar desire to inspect these areas of my body, especially since I was seated on the backseat of a taxi. I didn't understand what was happening to me. I didn't understand. I would have never thought I was capable of entertaining such revolting ideas.

As I sat, leaned forward on the seat, I began to detect a faint odor coming from the floor of the car. Though I wasn't able to place it directly, it seemed a sweet, sharp aromatic scent that resembled overly ripe, if not decaying, pomegranate or mango. I couldn't be sure which of the two fruit it was, but I found the scent agreeable nonetheless—agreeable in a strangely erotic way.

I sat up slowly and opened my eyes with care, allowing them to adjust to the sunlight before trying to focus them. Sunlight lay everywhere. The day was beautiful and brilliant; the sort of day I would've relished under pleasant circumstances. To my surprise, my head felt better at my having sat up. I crossed my forearms over my waist and began, for the first time since entering the taxi, taking stock of my surroundings. Before I could make a proper assessment, however, the driver spoke to me, allowing himself to emerge from obscurity.

"Are you okay, sir?"

I heard his question but didn't place much importance on it. It was a commonly heard question in New York but, being a reacclimatized New Yorker, I knew that questions of its variety from strangers usually were perfunctory and didn't require, nor did they deserve or carry an expectation of, a sincere response. I delivered the expected perfunctory answer.

"Yeah, I'm all right. Thanks."

"If you insist, sir. But to me you appear as a man who has just lost his girlfriend. That look of yours is quite telling, sir."

"*What?*" Anxiety wafted through me at the brush of his words. As he spoke, I noticed that the smell of overly ripe fruit grew more distinct. It was unquestionably the smell of mangos. Decaying mangos. *"What* did you say? Why would you say *that?"*

He didn't answer. I looked up into the rearview mirror in an attempt to make eye contact with him, to read his face, but he looked directly ahead at the road and didn't meet my eyes. I observed him closely. Tchaikovsky's, *Pathétique* played softly on the radio, replacing the nerve-razing rattle from the boot of the car. *Pathétique*—the death song.

He was a middle-aged man with a dark complexion I associated with the Middle East. Judging from his accent, I would have placed him somewhere in Pakistan or India, but I couldn't be sure. He wore a white turban, delicately folded, and he had a thin, well-manicured beard and mustache. A pair of silver-framed spectacles rested on the bridge of his nose, giving him a bookish look, and to my dismay, his physiognomy was disquietingly serious.

I continued to observe him and felt myself becoming increasingly agitated in the process. Though I distinctly remembered the black Lincoln Town Car to be the taxi I entered when I left home, I did not immediately recall this person to be the driver I met when I first took seat. That was nothing exceptional; people rarely remember the faces of those who drive them about in taxis. The white turban, however, should have stood out, I thought. But I simply couldn't remember it.

The driver spoke. "You know, there are many things in this world that can be seen but, study them as long as we like, we will never understand them. Why then do we try to understand the universe, which we cannot see?"

I again noticed the smell of decaying mangos filling the air. There was something about this man I found unnerving. I spoke to him whilst looking intently into his eyes as they were reflected in the rearview mirror.

"Oh, I'm sorry. Was that rhetorical question for *me?*" I began while trying to compose myself. "Well, tell me, since you *seem* to be a literary man, what's the point in asking such questions when the greatest thinkers the world has ever seen have already thrashed them out? What's wrong with possessing a desire to know?"

"Precisely my point, sir. The greatest minds the world has ever known have indeed thrashed them out, as you put it, sir, and still there is no answer." As he said this, the driver nodded his head in a quiet triumphant gesture at having used my own words to strengthen his thesis. There was something masterful in the way he spoke, in the calm manner in which he delivered his words, that caused me to surrender any inclination I may have harbored to spar with him mentally or employ sophist argument.

"You then ask *What is wrong* with possessing a desire to know?' Well, wouldn't it appear that possessing a desire to know the unknowable is inherently problematic, sir? Wouldn't you agree, sir? Look how easily you stumble."

The driver looked into the rearview mirror at me for the first time since our conversation had begun. His eyes were a cold, unearthly gray and seemed to penetrate my very essence. I drew back into my seat, away from him.

"Where are you from?" I inquired with disquiet. It was the only thing I could think to ask.

"*From?*"

"Yes, where are you from? Where were you born?

"Oh, I see. You know it as Kashmir."

"Oh, Kashmir," I replied with great interest. "Are you in Indian or Pakistani-held territory? And what's your name?" I was eager to change the subject and bring some sense of normalcy to the conversation. I was desperate to stabilize myself.

"Oh, what do these things matter?" the driver scoffed in amusement. I sensed a tinge of annoyance in his tone. I didn't speak, so he continued.

"These things, names and places, do not matter. They

are inconsequential. You shouldn't get caught up in them. I can ask you your name, but I know you will not give me your true name. And, why? Simply because you do not yet know your true name. Instead, you will think of the name your mother chose for you. Even then, you will not tell me *that* name because you are ashamed of it. You will, instead, give me a name that you have chosen for yourself. Am I right, sir?

"You, who seek to know the unknowable, ask me such trivial things. If I told you that right now as we speak, I am sitting by the Indus River thinking of that noble but dying river to the east and how to save it, you would not believe me. And why? Because your mind is closed. You, who seek to know the unknowable, have your eyes open, but keep your mind closed. I tell you, such things as names and places do not matter. These things change. What matters are *time* and *space*. These things will not change."

I was stunned. Questions deluged my mind, impacting and testing to their breaking points the levees of control I'd erected over time; the levees of discipline and self-containment. It was obvious to me now that this individual knew things about me—deeply personal things. But, I couldn't imagine how. I wanted to drill him, to question him, to get answers from him that would settle me, but I knew he would never submit to any form of interrogation. This man was not the sort. I could sense that.

Sitting there, paralyzed and speechless, I felt myself being examined; opened and examined by some probing force that somehow flowed from the driver. My inner workings—my thoughts and desires, fears and uncertainties—were exposed. So fully exposed and thoroughly examined I was, so naked, that it seemed utterly pointless to attempt to mask anything, to attempt to

13

hide. It was as if great spotlights shone on me, illuminating all that I was, everything I had ever done and thought of doing, everywhere I had been and desired to go, and revealing it all to the world; for anyone who might care to simply have a look. I felt shamefully exposed. Exposed and violated. The great spotlights had revealed not only *me* and all that *I* was, but also anywhere I may have thought to hide. Though I had no criminal past or secrets that would've proved damaging if they were revealed, the shame and nakedness I felt at that moment, of being so totally seen, were enough for me to consider, for an instant, killing the driver. In fact, if we hadn't been in a moving taxi, I'm almost sure that, at that instant, I would've tried.

I composed myself, to the extent possible, and found myself speaking as a man who had been caught committing a disgusting crime. I kept my eyes focused keenly on the driver.

"Well, there it is then. You seem to know a great deal about me. What do you know of the person I'm on my way to see? Is she all right?"

"Ahh. Again, this woman plagues your mind. You must love her a great deal, sir. Do you indeed?" The driver questioned me with a pleased expression and intonation. He obviously was more interested in my concern for "this woman" than in answering any of my questions.

"*Love her?*" I repeated in a low, feeling voice. "Her blood speaks to me from her veins."

"Ahh. Yes, there *is* that. But how do you know *that* is love, sir?"

"Well, I guess it's like the songwriter, Joni Mitchell, said, 'it's that dizzy, dancing way that you feel.'"

The driver nodded contemplatively but did not respond. His lips bore the faint impressions of an

14

impending smile, impressions so diminutive in their composition that he couldn't, himself, have been aware he possessed them.

I again inquired. "But tell me, please. Is she okay? I need to know." At this point, I had given up any hold I had on reason and empirical thought. I had simply abandoned them. I let them go without compunction or regret. At this moment, I just didn't care for them. I didn't care.

"Sir. These questions I cannot answer, but I will ask *you* this: Does her blood speak to you now?"

Once again, the driver gazed into his rearview mirror at me. It was the second time he had done so. His eyes were still an ethereal gray, but for some reason they didn't repel me as before. Unlike his voice, however, I noted his eyes were devoid, perhaps even incapable, of compassion.

"No. Her voice no longer reaches me. I cannot hear its call."

"Then, sir, that is the answer you seek to your question. The truth resides in *you* and speaks to you. You must learn to understand its voice and trust its direction."

The driver's words filled me with angst but, I thoroughly understood their meaning. There was no point in going on about Tiari now. It would have been tedious. I addressed the driver once again with a different subject.

"You know, I happen to know a little about this Indus River you speak of. If you speak of a dying river to the east of it, that puts you sitting by the Indus at about 2500 to 1900 B.C., or thereabouts. Is this what you're telling me?"

"*B.C.,* sir?"

"Yes, before Christ."

"*Christ,* sir?"

I was perplexed by his confusion. I couldn't tell whether it was genuine or not. I studied him more closely in the rearview mirror.

"Yes, Christ. Jesus Christ. If you know of Kashmir, and are indeed from there, you must have heard that name."

"Ahh, again you speak of names and places, sir. I tell you, again, that names and places do not matter. You do not even know your true name. You *cannot* know it, sir. There is no thing found on this earth that can reproduce the sound of your true name. Or mine. Even if I were to say your true name to you, you would not hear it, sir. You *could not* hear it. Do you understand? So, this Jesus Christ you speak of does not matter. You should forget this name, sir. You should forget *all* such names."

"There are a great number of people who would skin your hide if they heard you say that, mate." I spoke with greater ease now, even though a part of me was dismayed by his words. "You disappoint me. When you instruct to discard names such as Jesus Christ, I thought you would argue, as I: that the world has evolved sufficiently to warrant the ushering out of outmoded concepts such as religion and race, which have outlived their usefulness, if indeed they ever had any, but continue to burrow into modernity to risk the extinction of our species.

"I was prepared to hear you argue that since globalization has diminished the sovereignty and efficacy of the nation-state and brought an unprecedented interdependence, the only way to avoid a true clash of civilizations is to cast a new world order—one without religion. One without the myth of race. I believe human evolution will remain stalled until such a time."

The driver nodded energetically at my words whilst displaying a broad grin. Something I said had tickled him.

"Your understanding of where the world is and what is to come is exhaustive," he said. "I only add, with regards

16

to their hardened faces: do not fear them, sir. One who has sight cannot fear the blind. This Jesus you speak of is one of us. He is one *like* you and me, and his light shines like ours. He understands time and space, though *you* will come to understand. *He* does not fear the blind. I ask you, sir, if I send my child to school and he falls in love with his teacher, so much so that he forgets his lessons, what good does it do me? What good does it do the child? Is the teacher pleased?"

"I see your point," I conceded, whilst, again, moving closer to him. "You speak as though you know Jesus. Do you?" I asked, feeling utterly ridiculous as the words left me. The driver looked at me for the third time in the rearview mirror. This time, his eyes had a terribleness to them. I shrank back into the seat, knowing in an instant that I'd crossed a line. He spoke to me and I felt a familiar chill encase my body.

"Sir, the time has come. We must not allow the future, the past, and the present to meet as one in this way."

Instinctively, I leaned forward and peered through the taxi's windshield at the road ahead. There seemed to be some disturbance in the traffic approximately five hundred feet ahead of us. As we drew nearer, I could see the traffic accident in progress, and from the looks of it, it appeared to be a terribly awful thing that was playing out. It seemed, from my vantage point, that a white Lexus sedan and a black Lincoln Town Car similar to the one in which I was riding, had somehow collided and were beginning to spin and careen out of control just south of the Houston Street exit. The Lexus, having hit the highway partition, looked as though it was certain to overturn. A fatality seemed imminent. The driver and I, being so close to the event that was unfolding, and traveling at our speed, were poised

17

for a collision with the capsizing Lexus. A lump formed in my throat. It was all happening rather quickly.

"That, sir, is the future. We must leave."

*   *   *

"I had that dream again last night."

"Which one?"

"The one where I'm living the last two days of my life but don't know it. Only I *do* know it, 'cause somewhere in my head I know I've had the dream before."

The room gets quiet again. With the exception of a radio playing classical music softly in the background, the room manages to maintain its deathly calm. It always does since the doctor never readily engages on the heels of my statements when I stop speaking—as *normal* interlocutors do. She always waits to see if I have more to say. So, I don't say anything. I just keep playing with the lighter in my right hand, wanting to light up a fag.

"Does anything happen differently in *this* dream?" I hear her voice but can't see her. She's sitting out of sight in that overstuffed leather chair of hers. I'm lying on the sofa looking at the wall that has all her great and fabulous diplomas on it. *Dr. Tiari Cheng, Tiari Cheng, MD., Tiari Cheng, PhD. University of this. Graduate of that.*

"Yeah. The driver talks to me this time."

The *death silence* enters the room.

"What does he say?"

I can smell her perfume. It's faint and I gather it's because she doesn't want to be any more distracting than she naturally is, being the beautiful woman she is. But, I detect its distinct aroma in the air.

"He said I didn't even know my true name."

The death silence swells. Beethoven's, *Moonlight Sonata* is beginning to wind itself down on the radio. I note how the maestro's work speaks with a particularly eerie voice in *this* room.

"Is that everything he said?" she asks.

"Yeah."

The tiny rustling of papers in her lap presses the silence back. She's checking her notes. The room is small with dark wall paneling along three walls and books aplenty in the ceiling high bookcase covering the entire remaining wall. Stylish as she appears to be, she's chosen a plush neutral colored carpet instead of the more fashionable choice—a dark hardwood floor. My hand has become sweaty but I keep on fidgeting with my lighter, wanting to smoke a fag real bad.

"So, did you hear your mother's voice in this dream as well?" she asked me after what seemed to me to be a measured pause. "Is she still reciting the same childhood rhyme to calm you?"

"Yeah."

"Have you had any thoughts since we last met about who the crying child might be? Or, thoughts about who was trying to call you on the telephone?"

"No."

Silence. Beethoven's, *Moonlight Sonata* is finally ending and I'm glad of it.

"Speaking of telephones, I see you're holding a cigarette lighter today. Have you taken up smoking? It's usually your cellphone that you twiddle," she rejoins. The intonation of her voice betrays a smile. She's trying to relax me. She's obviously thinking that I'm playing with my lighter because I'm nervous. But, I'm not that simple.

"No, I don't smoke. I lost my mobile phone is all."

The room goes quiet again, but I have a thought. I line my words up and scrutinize them before setting them free.

"I think the kid that's crying might be me," I continue before she could ask why I would own a lighter if I didn't smoke. I hear her pen scratching against the pad. The wood paneling bends the inflection so that it resembles something like clawing. The fruity scent of her perfume remains adrift in the air. "Don't ask me why I feel that way; I just do. I dunno why."

Her pen continues its clawing against the pad.

"Hmm, you stated once before that, in the dream, you were *pulled* from the car you were riding in and *placed* in an identical car traveling some distance behind?" She inquired, seeking confirmation. But, she's reading the lines from her notes. I can sense it. The pitch of her voice always dips whenever she speaks while looking downward.

"Yeah."

"And from the car you were placed in, you witnessed your own death in a traffic accident ahead?"

"Yeah," I responded. Her understanding was impaired by *something*, but I didn't correct her. Simple reasoning would have indicated, had it been applied, that if I was pulled from the car, then I was no longer in it. Therefore, it couldn't have been *my* death I witnessed.

The death silence ruptures, permitting the opening bars of Tchaikovsky's, *Pathétique* to seep into the room from the radio. *Pathétique*. The maestro's final completed sympathy before his death seeps into the room. Its arrival chills me.

"Have you yet identified the color or make of the car that collided with the car you were taken from?" she seems genuinely interested. "In an earlier session you expressed that you were desperate to find this out."

"No."

She breathed in deeply which meant we were done for the day. She doesn't realize how telling she is in everything she does. It happens with people who are sincere. I know I'll miss her. She's really beautiful. I already begin to sit up on the sofa.

"Well, that ends us for today. We'll pick up again next week Friday. Same time?"

"Sure Doc," I replied. She stands up and, using the back of her hands, smoothens her white skirt against her thighs. A spring lily, to me, could not have been fresher. I wanted to hold the moment. "Where ya headed, Doc? Maybe I can give you a ride again, even part way?"

She smiles that tender smile of hers; I study it.

"No, but thanks. I finally bought a car. Just yesterday. I'm taking it up the coast this weekend for a little rest and relaxation. My parents have completed the installation of their pool and asked me up to visit," she turns and puts her papers on the chair behind her. I watch, but I don't interrupt her.

"I figure I'll go home," she continues. "I'll snooze a bit, then leave late tonight to beat the weekend rush. I'm hoping to be on the road by 2 AM if all goes well." She beams with delight. It's the usual parting small talk, but I can tell her happiness is authentic.

I force my own smile. "I bet the pool is heated."

"How did you know?" Her subtle fragrance will accompany me. Of this I'm certain. I stand and grab my denim jacket from off the chair by the door. She challenges me playfully. "Bet you can't guess what model car I bought?"

Pathétique fills the room.

21

I Am Per

The fluorescent bulbs hummed and crackled under
the strain to deliver what was to become the blinding,
intolerable light. Yes, the intolerably-blinding light that
confronted the room with undeserving malice and served
to aid my discomfort, was by my design. Somewhere in
the house, someone, a child, perhaps, sang some silly song;
again, to my discomfort.

The attic room I'd rented measured thirteen feet by
nine feet and had an eight-foot ceiling; the minimum legal
height for New York City, I once heard someone say. With
the exception of a sleeping bag I'd placed in the center
of the dusty hardwood floor, no other furniture existed
in the space. Here and there, unopened bottles of water
lay without regard alongside the emptied, crushed and
decrepit ones across the discolored oak where I'd placed, or
had inadvertently kicked them. I listened to the little girl's
song and noted that its silliness saddened me. It was true,
what I had always felt: To be free meant the artist must
live with lasting loneliness.

Here in the Brooklyn lodging I'd secured, I promised
the family that owned the house I'd use only fluorescent
bulbs in the four fixtures I'd had delivered to place in
each corner of the room. Surprisingly, they didn't press
me with questions regarding the need for the fixtures

and were amenable to me using them, providing I drew the curtains fully over the windows at nightfall and used no bulb over 100 watts. These caveats suited me, since complying with them would not cause my shadow to be produced in the place. It was my shadow, you see, that had become problematic. To this cryptic statement I'll add, only for the present, that my name is Per: Per Ingerson— poet and graduate student of Government at a prominent New York City university, which probity, in her wisdom, instructs me to leave unnamed. I am *Per*. I am a man. I am not nothing. My individuality is indelibly inscribed and ineradicably included in my identity. My identity is manifestly mine.

Two days ago something happened to me; something that brought occasion for me to consider all I thought I understood about the world, and of myself. A rather grand but sobering thing that began three days ago, on Friday, when I'd learned of a poetry reading that was to occur in the grand auditorium at school the following day at noon. Are you still with me?

Being a poet, I made the requisite inquiries and submitted registration documents allowing me to participate in the poetry reading. There was much I wanted to say about the political winds currently blowing in Washington in general and the myopic, pernicious bluster escaping from the Commander–in-Chief, specifically. Though received late, my registration was accepted by the administrators of the event—partly because of my notoriety on campus and partly due to my extraordinary gift of persuasion.

That evening, as I worked on the poem I would recite—a poem to end any debate as to the agenda of the

present American regime—I was nearly paralyzed by a
sense of foreboding. My mind was clear, but there was a
paranoia gyrating within me that seemed to intensify with
every pen stroke. Was it the words I wrote? Was it my
criticism of the present governing administration? My
damnation of a politically-polarized press that was once
free but was now, itself, a special interest enslaved by its
myriad of agendas; a press seeking power over trumpeting
the truth? Was the divestiture of dignity, the unmooring
of morality, the upending of poise and grace now to be the
norm in the upper echelons of government, and—dare I
say it—American society altogether? Was the individual
and his corresponding will to be brought to nothing unless
subsumed into a politically-identifiable group? And, if
these were so, why should writing about these bother me
now, when it never had before? I wondered about it, but
continued to write. I was being warned, it seemed, perhaps
by some inexplicable force in the universe. Could it be
that the government of the country I now lived in and its
presumed elected head were so powerful that even unseen
forces within the universe would bend to their will? I
chuckled at the notion, mocking the absurdity of my own
thoughts. After a short while, the feeling left me, replaced
by a surreal sense of being in two places at once; a sense
of myself being juxtaposed between the "here and now"
and an entirely different time and place; a place with a
dissolving definition of time.

I had a dream that night—an odd dream, to be sure.
In my dream, the poetry reading of the following day
was underway and I'd just concluded the recitation of
my poem as scheduled. Stretched before me, opposite my
podium, were the faces of students, vast as the blades of
grass in a rolling field. These faces, I remember, beamed

with euphoria when I'd first taken my place to speak. Such was their anticipation of my coming words. Such was their admiration of me.

Upon uttering the final words of my poem, a child approached me from stage left and handed me a cardboard box. The box measured thirteen inches, by nine inches, and was eight inches deep. I did not measure the box nor were there measurements written on the box that I could see. But somehow, details like these are known in dreams if they are meant to be. As I took the box from the child, I noted it was warm and did not have much weight; three pounds, or so, would have been my estimate. I took the box and laid it on the podium, giving the child a pleasant smile, which was greeted with mocking indifference—I took special note of that. The expressionless eyes of the audience never left me.

I unfolded the top flaps while observing the astonishingly loud echo the endeavor produced in the hall; such was the calamitous calm that accompanied the process. A glowing orange orb was the content. A sun. The earth's sun. There was little doubt in my mind of this. What struck me, however, was that the sinister sense of foreboding had returned.

With upturned palms, I scooped the sun from the box and held it at eye level. I saw my hands being consumed by the flames, but I did not feel the heat; not on my hands nor on my face. Turning to face the wall behind me I noted with some consternation that I produced no shadow. It was then I observed the child who'd given me the box. His face, and all the faces in the large hall, had turned ashen.

I replaced the sun inside the box and exited stage right, the thundering echo of my footfall resounding after me.

*　*　*

I awoke the following morning to an overarching despondency. The debilitating surreality I'd harnessed the evening before while writing my piece stayed connected to me. In the newness of the morning air, however, it seemed to deepen, leaving me with the inexplicable sense that I was fading. *Fading.*

While sitting for breakfast, I reconsidered the poem I was to deliver; the words I'd chosen, my harsh criticism of the ruling administration, my position concerning the perversion of the U.S. legal system by plutocrats and the various agendas constructed and in play by the most insidious members of American society, to bend the country towards an amoral identity and existence. I'll note here that the mere reconsideration of the reading of the poem diminished the oddness I felt. It was a striking, if not halting, communiqué; as if I were, again, being warned off the endeavor.

*　*　*

I recited my poem two days ago and swiftly exited the hall and then the building by a rear door to enhance the suggestion of humility. It was then, against the sun-soaked sidewalk, I first noticed the change.

The *change?* My shadow had *disconnected* from me; its feet beginning the elongated stretch of its black form on the pavement some thirteen inches or so, from where my soles met the asphalt. I was astonished at this, but also noted that the thing delayed in mimicking my movements

29

as though grudgingly complying with its fated mandate. I say "grudgingly," since this was the distinct impression I had at the time—that my shadow was growing hostile toward me and would soon wish me harm. I compared the behavior of my shadow to those of other people traveling on the same sidewalk as me. Mine was the only one disconnected in such a manner and delayed in its reaction to the movements of its source.

Placing my steps northward, I dismissed the observation and the conclusion I'd drawn from it as merely a consequence of the call for sleep—and I cut a mental path to the wine shop at the corner of Broadway and 108th Street, feeling the whole time that a line had been crossed by me that could not be revisited; that my circle contained a separation and was no longer complete.

I'll state up front, so you'll understand, that I'm not the sort of man who relies on alcohol, tobacco products or any such thing to calm me. However, though early in the day, I thought it appropriate to buy a bottle of scotch from the neighborhood spirits shop to aid, with a few sips, the long sleep I had planned.

Having purchased the scotch, I walked with a measured pace back to my apartment. The sun was still high in the mid-day sky. I noticed, now, that the space created by the disconnection of my shadow from me had widened, starting at a distance of a least two feet or more. Was the thing leaving me? Was I in good health?

The detour to the spirits shop had added at least twenty minutes to my trip back home. As I stepped from the sidewalk and into the doorway of my building, a belligerent curiosity caused me to turn and observe my final steps from the asphalt. My shadow had gone entirely.

I stepped back quickly to the center of the sidewalk, just
to be sure. There was no shadow for me as there was for
other passersby.

Overcome by feelings of disgust and humiliation,
I stepped again into my building before anyone could
notice the change that had occurred with my existence.
I had had enough of the sun, the dirty sidewalk and its
grotesque revelation, and of the cares and opinions I
held that unwittingly brought me to this position. Sleep
was what I wanted; a respite from the burdens that
political connectedness and socially engineered moral
disassociation had brought me. Scotch, I had. I firmly
grasped the bag that encased the bottle in my right hand.
The mechanical hierocracy of the elevator's machinery
murmured overhead. My body ascended. But all else, all
that mattered, bowed to lap up the ugly degradation that
was now the life force and identity of Western existence.
My soul was dark at this moment and I detected bitterness
in what should have been my quiet inner space when I
acknowledged the resident darkness.

I entered my apartment, opened the scotch, and despite
my earlier intention to mix a light cocktail or sip a shot,
proceeded to drink the undiluted darkness directly from
the bottle, tacitly wishing to harm myself at that moment
by the very act. The burning I felt in my throat and chest
reminded me of the heat I did not feel when I'd removed
the sun from its carton and held it to my face in my dream
the night prior. Unsure how much I'd gulped while
standing at my doorway, I placed the open bottle down on
the coffee table and threw myself on the sofa, lying there
on my back while facing the door I'd just passed through
and ignoring the window behind my head. Self-loathing
was the feeling I identified in myself as I stared at the

ceiling. Something profound and necessary had left me, I thought. My shadow was the first to go—but, perhaps, not the last.

And then I slept—a tortured and ambiguous sleep that only yielded the satirical rest reserved for unloved children and evil men. "The sleep of the damned", my dear mother used to call it. I dreamt an odd dream there that seemed, by its opening mood, to be a continuation of the dream I'd had the night prior.

In this dream the great hall where I had recited my poem had returned. The cardboard box containing the sun sat on the podium where I had left it. The still and ashen faces of the audience also remained, precisely as I had last seen them. The knotting silence returned to attendance, stifling in its complexity and also as I'd remembered it. Nothing in the place had changed since my departure and it was clear now that my dream of the previous night had resumed.

The child who'd given me the box re-emerged from stage left and approached the podium as before. With reservation, I observed it more closely now while simultaneously noting that my dream continued in the first person—though I knew I was not in that place. The only way I could explain this inscrutable ennui that had again taken over me was that it was somehow woven into that sensation I'd previously experienced of being juxtaposed with myself in another place and time, as obscure and as diffused as that time might have been. An abject bending of one's self occurs in dreams, I understood, so my dream's continuation in the first person, despite my absence (I reassured myself) was normal, since it's in the first person that the mind sees the world. But to see a room where one is simultaneously both absent and present disturbs the mind, even in dreams.

The child was female, I think, and around seven-years-old. The creature was unnaturally slender in frame, and was frighteningly frail. My observations stopped here when I noticed the ashen skin and the wide black eyes that did not (or could not) blink its accompanying eyelids (assuming the thin black lines above the dark holes could be called that). My absent self backed away from the child at that moment and watched as it removed the box from the podium and placed it on the floor, as if setting an example. It opened the flaps and the glow of the enclosed sun escaped and reflected on its face and on the ashen faces of all who sat in the great hall. The unfolding of the flaps, again, echoed throughout the space.

At that moment, the child stepped into the box and descended into it, folding closed the flaps over its head to disappear entirely from view. The audience exulted in mirthless laughter. For my part, the oddness of the occurrence—given the size of the box and the unnerving thinness of the child—signaled an ominous event. The box was intended for me. It was given to *me*. So, the descent should have been mine. But, descent into *what*? The entire scene upsets me still when I reflect upon it.

*   *   *

I awoke unrested and without a sense of the time or how long I had slept. A darkened sky looming behind my window, with a large, spherical moon framed tidily within its single pane was the only reference my senses would afford me. Moonlight filled the room and lit the wall opposite the window brilliantly. On this wall and the entrance door that shared it, the shadow of a floor lamp and one of the whiskey bottle standing on the coffee table passed without significance under my lazy gaze. Immediately to the left of these two objects stood the shadow of a person with arms akimbo. I noticed the thing amidst a mental fog that sometimes descends on fatigued minds—and I saw no particular importance to it until the oddity, within a few seconds, called my mind to focus: The shadow of a person is caused by a person.

Quickly shifting to a sitting position, I turned to look behind me to see what person was standing at my window. There was no one. And since my window was not served by a balcony or fire escape, whatever person there might have been would have been standing inside my apartment. But there was no one there. I turned again to the wall in time to capture the final movement of the shadow as it dashed with a crouching posture into the darkness at the right side of the room and was hidden from me. Stunned, I remained seated while peering into that darkness, hoping, I suppose, that the thing would again show itself or give some other indication to my mind of what it was. Goose bumps rose on my arms.

The room was quiet. The streets outside, my mind told me, were abnormally quiet. I believed this to be the case and slowly rose from my slumbering place, searching with veiled vision the darkened areas of the room as I did. I was not alone. The longer I peered into the blackness, the more convinced I was of this. I began a careful move toward the light switch next to the entrance doorway. The timidity of my beginning steps was a revelation to me in that darkened space. Terror had nearly immobilized me. I collected my fragmented will and with a driven determination, moved toward the light switch.

"Don't," a voice came. A male voice, low and whispery. "Don't. Or I'll kill you. I will kill you where you stand."

The voice came from the darkened area of the room that was to the right of the wall lit by the moonlight. But because of the brilliantly moonlit wall, my eyes could not properly acclimate to the darkened side. As a consequence, this area was impenetrable by sight—so I stood, frozen, listening to the belligerent blackness. The silence continued for an indeterminable period and I felt certain that I was being studied by some entity shrouded in the dark.

The voice, I noted mentally, was calm but not genuinely so. Behind its words was an unmoored spirit; the spirit of an individual disassociated and internally distressed.

"Do you know who I am?" the voice asked in its whispery way after some time. The deceitful calm in the question further unnerved me. So much so that I thought I would fall. My legs had become weak beneath me.

"No," I replied feebly.

"Do you know *what* I am?"

I spoke as a condemned man from whom hope had been withdrawn. My voice was small.

"No."

The silence returned for another indeterminable period. I was still being studied.

"I see," the voice rejoined flatly, without concern. "You should sit".

Slowly, I sat, but now in an upright position toward the edge of the cushion, as would a person prepared to spring into some action. My palms rested on my knees.

"I tell you again, I will kill you. Without hesitation."

His words were both a warning and verification that I was, indeed, being keenly observed. My body language had provoked the admonition. I addressed the matter quickly to quell his growing agitation.

"I understand. I won't do *anything* unless you tell me to," I paused here, thinking he would interject—but he did not. I continued carefully. "Who are you? What do you want?"

Again, silence greeted my inquiries. Before continuing, I examined my selected words for signs of distress. I wanted to communicate neither fear nor aggression in the words I'd chosen, nor the tone in which I delivered them.

"Have I harmed you in some way? If so, I'm sorry. How did you get into my apartment?"

His reply came more quickly than I had to this point grown accustomed. Suppressing the urge to look around the room, I continued to train my eyes on the discoursing darkness.

"I know you," he answered. "You're part of a problematic group. I've followed your movements for a while now."

I listened intently as he spoke, waiting for some clue as to what this was all about. He continued in his sadistically steady way.

"Do you think you're some kind of god? Or, some kind of mythical creature with the preeminent light of understanding?" He paused for a moment, as if to draw breath—though I heard none drawn. "I bet you'd like it if I called you *Your Eminence?*" He paused again, briefly. "Alright, then."

His expression moved like the contentious undercurrent of a beguilingly calm sea. This was a man,

I felt, who had already murdered me many times in his heart. I trusted his threatening words and doubted nothing of the precariousness of my situation. He was no ordinary intruder, hoping to lay hands on my scant belongings. To consume my essence—to undo me—was the intention behind his intrusion; perhaps, even, the reason for his existence. Why he delayed in delivering the destruction drawn in his designs I couldn't understand, but I attached no advantage to this eventuality. He simply could have been mulling the moment, savoring the scent of my fear.

Certainly, he was a masterful speaker, and was accustomed to orating such malevolent pronouncements. It followed, then, that a mind accustomed to producing masterful speech was no stranger to higher thought and to the formulation and dissemination of ideas. Barring the idea that this mind was utterly mad (which was something I couldn't wholly rule out) this seemed a reasonable path to lengthen the speaker's delay and even, as newly-found hope would introduce it, to reposition his feet on a course away from me.

"You can call me whatever you wish," I started. "Even though you mock me, I will answer you." I measured my words and balanced my intonation and delivery, so that my intentions were not implied. I wanted to tease him out, but not anger him; to engage him in conversation and change the way our stage was presently set and to put me in a less-cowering posture.

"I will not call you *Your Eminence*," He exhorted, seeming to bristle at the mere thought of letting the words pass his lips.

"Well. It was *your* suggestion," I followed.

"Never mind that."

I paused here. Partly for effect and partly owing to a cunningness I felt rising within me. Fear was gradually being displaced.

"And what should I call *you*?" I rejoined.

Another briefer pause ensued. This one, I felt acutely, was different from its predecessor in that I sensed a manipulative shrewdness was being employed in the darkness. He answered with a note that seemed tentatively pressed.

"It doesn't matter. If you start talking, you're obviously talking to *me*. No need to call my attention."

"Not necessarily," I replied plainly, but with an appreciative chuckle. There was, in fact, calculation being employed in the pause, as I had suspected. What angle was he playing? "I could be speaking to myself. I am prone to doing that."

"You think I'm an intruder. Why would I give you any part of my name?"

I examined his response for evidence of disingenuousness, but found none. "I simply thought that since we were speaking as gentlemen that we'd follow convention and trade names. I haven't called you an intruder, have I? I am *Per*. Initials would suffice, given the circumstances."

"I.D. In the lower case if you please."

"I see. Very well." He had me stumped. "But I'm sorry. I don't know how to speak in lower case. Is that what you mean?"

"Yes. I know you don't. That's part of your problem. You can call me whatever you wish. I will answer you."

"Oh. Very well," He'd returned my previous reply to me and vexed me by doing so. "How long will you ride this carousel, Id?" In annoyance, I'd pronounced out his initials and lobbed it at him in ridicule. "I was under the impression that you'd come to harm me. Now I see you've come to either tickle my sides or to irritate me."

"This carousel will presently become a spinning wheel for the threads of truth. Or, a pretty rope to ring your lying neck."

I did not respond. The singularly sinister undertow of his threat suggested that a specific action on his part had already been decided. Briefly glancing at the whiskey bottle on the coffee table before me, I wondered if I was not dreaming the dream of drunks. I did not *feel* drunk, but drunk men do not feel drunk in their drunken dreams. They feel terror. Terror of the monsters and of the other-worldly creatures that visit them from the shadowy areas of their tormented minds.

I became agitated at the sight of the whiskey bottle. Unlike normal nightmares, where terrible things hidden in the darkness mark the entirety of the nightmare, in drunken dreams terrible things concealed in the darkness do not remain concealed, but are more terrible once they inevitably move into the light. This realization enraptured me and I sprang up and grabbed the opened whiskey bottle by the neck and hurled it into the darkness—and at the voice encased within. Some noise unlike the sound of a shattering bottle reached me. I stood, ready for the charge of a beast or monster from the disturbed darkness; for the attack of some demonic dog-man or other grotesque entity my drunk and tormented mind could meld together to mangle me. I stood ready, but nothing advanced except a steady voice with its promise of my undoing in its fabric.

"You're a fool. And now—," he paused here. "I will make my feast on your foolish and cowardly heart. I warned you."

Instinctively, I dashed to the door before my path could be cut off and fumbled with the lock while feverishly yanking on the doorknob. My back faced the room, but anticipating an assailant who would soon be in reach of me, I abruptly turned while passing my hand quickly over the light switch, which was now to the left of me. Across the yellow, light-filled room, the displaced darkness revealed its recesses. Apart from the whiskey bottle that had smashed through the television's glass front, there was nothing else amiss on that side of the room. There was no evil conspirator, crouching. No murderous weapons, abandoned. Nothing at all to harm me—except, of course, the bottle of whiskey I'd purchased with the intention of harming myself; a weapon I had instead used against the television.

I was stunned and confused. I stood at the door for a short time, debating whether I should stay in the apartment or leave. Finally, I decided to leave. The circle of my life was losing its integrity, and the shattered television stood as a warning to me to be mindful of myself. I exited the apartment and the mess I'd made, determining I'd deal with them at some later time.

*

My meandering walk took me to a public bench on Riverside Drive near 120th Street and not far from the university I attend. Having sat and stared endlessly across the waters of the Hudson, I could scarcely remember the path I'd taken to get there or anything I'd seen along the way. It was a clear night, I remember. The way an eerily-large moon hung in the sky and reflected off the water like a flame struck me as profound. The crisp predawn air caused my eyes to tear. And in whatever direction I looked, emptiness and solitude sighed. Loneliness is a negating anti-person, I thought. As real in the universe as dark matter and equally unseeable. I imagined it wasn't long after three in the morning.

For a long while, I sat there and thought about it all, questioning whether or not I was going mad. I had spoken to someone hiding in the darkness of my apartment. This was certain. And this individual had spoken to me. This was fact. Or was it? Several times I tried to accept the explanation that I had awoken from a dream and launched into a hallucination instigated by fatigue and alcohol. This explanation seemed rational—but I was reluctant to embrace it.

I sat there, but in time, the hardness of the bench made me uncomfortable. I stood to stretch and noticed that, though I stood in the glow of a streetlight beside my bench, I, again, did not cast a shadow, though the bench itself did. This was proof to me that what I'd experienced earlier in the day was no trick of the sun and was not some atmospheric aberration as an earlier thought suggested.

I was in danger and felt it palpably. And as completely cloaked in this danger as I was, it seemed as if no power or entity on earth could release me from it. And as astounding and as out of place as it may seem, a penetrating and nagging question confronted me at that moment: When a tree is cut and falls in a forest, is the tree dying from the moment it is felled, or is it actually dead from that very instant and beginning its first steps of decay, however imperceptible.

This question teased me closer to mental paralysis

because it was connected to a larger and more consequential one that was, in fact, directly connected to *me*. This larger question of a man whose heart had failed and who required the use of a machine to circulate his blood, dogged me with its advance. Though this wasn't precisely the same question as the tree, it held me because it sprung from the tangential thread. Like the tree that was cut off from its natural anchor to existence, wasn't this man, whether conscious or unconscious, thinking or unthinking, already truly dead? The short answer my mind afforded was that the machine, an unnatural thing, stood in substitution for the man's natural anchor thereby transforming his existence to an unnatural thing—a thing that does not comply with the natural order of life as established. Wasn't I, then, a man who could not cast a shadow, as unnatural as my situationally reasoned man? Wasn't I separated from my natural anchor to a spiritual existence and therefore dead? What did it mean, then, to be *alive*?

I drew a breath and readied myself to return to my apartment, though not really wanting to. As I turned toward the street, to leave this public seating area, my peripheral vision, aided by the light over a distant bench, registered a dark form as it darted ten feet or so from that bench and toward the street I would soon cross. The form disappeared into a darkness, lingering there and failing to reappear on the lighted sidewalk as its trajectory would suggest it should. Whoever it was, my mind told me, chose to remain in the darkness. I watched for a short time without moving, then hastened my steps to the sidewalk, crossed the road and continued down a well-lit perpendicular street, where an accumulation of people on the corner at its further end could be seen.

I don't recall the name of the street. However, I do recall the block having an abundance of saplings planted on both sides of the road, and that these were responsible for the street being unusually bright, owing to the trees' inability to provide adequate cover from the streetlights. Despite the youth of the trees, I observed they still cast a short shadow, appropriate to their size, along the tops of the cars parked near them and on the sidewalk surrounding them.

With certainty, I knew I was being pursued. The glancing glimpse of a crouching dark form dashing to the shadow of a nearby tree for sanctuary or to a darkened crevice of a house's front garden convinced me of this. I moved with determination toward the small gathering of people at the corner, discerning as I drew closer, the establishment there to be a pub with a few patrons standing outside it to smoke and chat for a time. I slowed my pace as I drew near the people and though not attempting to fit in to their groupings, stood loosely among them to turn and nonchalantly survey the street I'd just travelled.

Almost immediately, a stout and gruff-looking man about my age and with thick red hair, beard and mustache stepped into the doorway from inside the pub. He emerged holding an opened bottle of beer, but I gave no thought to him until he spoke loudly at me and startled me. His heavy Irish accent punctuated his abrasiveness.

"Oye! Where's ya shadow ya clatty wretch?!"

He stood in the doorway, glaring at me. The others on the sidewalk turned to examine me but could not yet make sense of the outburst.

"Oye! Oye! What?!" The red haired man continued.

"Ya from the devil are ya? Ya better fook off 'fore I sort ya out! Back to the devil wit' ya!"

Another man, just then, came up behind him and took him gently by the shoulders from the door. I heard him speak. "Get away from the door, ya drunk fool, 'fore ya get us all in with the police."

With the red-bearded man secured inside, I felt I was now being more intensely-scrutinized by the patrons standing on the sidewalk. Their faces betrayed a confusion as the realization set in that I was the only one among them on the sidewalk without some sort of shadow. I walked away quickly before any further unpleasantness could erupt, and as I did so, I heard one in the group say to his companions: "Shit, man. That guy is fucked." And another reply, "Fucked is just the beginning for that one, mate."

My legs ached at the panicked pace of my walking. I was anxious to return to my apartment, yet in dread of being there. But there was no place else to go. The city, as large and as populated as it was, had always seemed to me disentangled from the cares of its residents. I felt this way now, more so than ever. My silent stalker continued in his pursuit behind me for the two additional blocks I'd travelled since stopping at the pub. So clumsy were his attempts to conceal himself that the thought occurred to me that his clumsiness may have been deliberate—a clever attempt to unnerve me and make me psychologically unconstituted for his inevitable attack.

But who was he? What did he want with *me*? And as difficult as it would be for anyone I might tell this narrative to believe me, it was at this point, for the first time, the question approached my mind, whether this individual was the one in my apartment earlier that evening—the person I'd spoken to and who had threatened to kill me.

I had to have been going mad, I thought. In truth, I'd not seen a person at all. I'd *heard* one, yes. But many factors could have contributed to that, I reasoned, though I couldn't clearly identify one of those factors. But it was not a *person* that I saw. The suggestion of a person—a shadow, is all I could admit to witnessing.

Now, there was this *thing* that pursued me. I say *thing* because, again, as many times as I'd turned to survey the street behind my steps, I had never seen a person. In fact, judging by the way the thing moved—in this style of crouching and darting into shadowy places to hide, some of these places small, low, and difficult to access, and darting into them in such a manner that showed no regard for injury, I conjectured that this was not a person. No person could move this way. Of course, there was also the question of my detached shadow that commanded contemplation. What had become of it? Or, perhaps the question I should ask is what had become of *me* that I should cast no shadow? Had I not been seen, examined and spoken to by the patrons at the pub, I would now possibly question my own existence.

It then occurred to me that at some point I had stopped my movement and was standing as a statue on the pavement, pondering my ideas and questioning the sanity of my thoughts. A strange sight I must have been to anyone chancing to see me at that hour. As I resumed my steps, I noticed a convenience store at the corner of the block, its bright interior lights spilling out onto the sidewalk through its oversized windows, signaling the merchant was a 24-hour establishment. Coming closer to it, I realized that the entrance was around the corner on the street perpendicular, and would not have been visible by my pursuer yet. I thought to move quickly around the corner in a wide pivot away from the shop so as not to clue my pursuer of my intent, then reverse course quickly to enter the shop and conceal myself, if possible—but in a way that would allow me to see outside.

Positioning myself behind a row of hot coffee dispensers that were tall enough on their tables to prevent me from being seen from the street, I spotted something that made my blood beat cold. Peering through a gap between two of the coffee dispensers, ambling flat along the sidewalk, I saw—a shadow. It turned the corner with seeming haste and travelled down the sidewalk in a path I led it to believe I had taken. A *shadow*—dark and elongated across the pavement. The shadow of a person but without the requisite person.

In my astonishment, I must have allowed some odd sound to escape me because the store's clerk, from his position behind the counter, stirred and began looking at me rather inquisitively. I returned his gaze as nonchalantly as I could but peered again outside when the shadow reappeared and stood across the sidewalk in front of the doorway, as if perplexed. Though I can't say why I held this impression, it was unquestionably the way I'd interpreted it.

"Hey," I heard a male voice say. "You need help?" It was the clerk and I understood his question to be the sort that seeks to decode a person and not a sincere offer of assistance. I was reluctant to answer him for fear of divulging my whereabouts to the shadow now pacing the sidewalk directly in front of the store. But I knew that if I didn't submit *some* sort of response the clerk would only become more suspicious. I put an empty coffee cup to my lips and pretended to taste the coffee I'd just prepared, while gesturing silently with my left hand that I didn't need help. Seemingly satisfied with my response, the man ended his examination of me and returned his attention to whatever held it previously. I looked at the sidewalk once more and happened to see the shadow move diagonally across the wide empty intersection, away from the store. The importance of its movement escaped me until the realization came that my apartment lay in that direction.

Needless to say, I didn't dare go home. However, alternative lodgings after 3 AM in New York City was a challenge. I had no friends I could call, so a hotel was my only option. A hotel in Brooklyn, I reasoned, would probably be more economically representative of self.

I closed the matter in my mind and set a course of action. Still holding the empty coffee cup, I browsed the convenience store looking for the place where newspapers and other printed publications were gathered. A crudely-constructed wooden bench by the door satisfied my search with its offerings of stained, day-old newspapers, promotional fliers and similar items placed on it. Among these items were a few thin real estate catalogs, printed on cheap recycled paper and each boasting local listings of houses and apartments for rent or sale. The catalogs with the listings for Brooklyn and Queens were among these and caught my eye. Being free of charge, I picked up the Brooklyn catalog and held it up to the store's clerk to show my hand.

"Tasted the coffee, brother. Burned," I lied and exited the store, taking nothing of value but owing them, quite possibly, my life.

*

The taxi driver dropped me off in front of a small but newly-constructed hotel in Brooklyn, situated at the foot of the Manhattan Bridge. My instruction to the white-turbaned driver had been to take me to the nearest hotel in Brooklyn that wasn't known to be expensive—though, in retrospect, I can't imagine how he could have known the prices of hotel rooms or why, in the moment, I thought he would. As it was, I carried no cash and my credit cards had space enough for only a modest and short existence away from home. I paid the taxi's fare with one of these cards.

I checked in, bought two candy bars from a vending machine in the hotel's lobby (it accepted credit cards, to my surprise), and proceeded to my room: Room 315. Once there, I kicked off my shoes just inside the door, gave the room a cursory inspection, and fell face-down onto the king-sized bed. Sleep quickly approached from some inscrutable corner of my being. I hoped my nemesis would not be as successful in finding me. That thought dogged me a moment, though I soon let it go and surrendered my essence to the clawing night.

*

I dreamt a dream that night. A dreadful dream it was, I remember, though in retrospect, I cannot understand why my *self* in the dream was so alarmed and my dreaming mind was so impacted.

The box the child had descended into in my stead in my previous dream had returned. I recognized it without doubt, having held and examined it closely in the first dream. In this latest dream, however, the box reappeared, first hovering in an unbounded white expanse of nothingness that gave its definition a stark clarity. After a moment, colors and forms began to take shape, finding their place in the expanse—first, as faded watercolors might appear on a canvas, then becoming a darker and more complex image.

I recognized the room coming into form before the picture had coalesced on that canvas of white expanse. Like a white napkin placed lightly over spilled ink, different areas of the canvas bled through with replete three dimensional colors and shapes. The room coming into view, I had seen countless times in photos and news streams over many years but despite its importance had always struck me as distant and disconnected from wherever I stood; the visual equivalent of white noise to a mind searching for answers. The two lengthy cloth sofas facing each other were situated toward one end of the oval floor and they counter-balanced the large partners desk at the opposite end of that floor. Stately windows and two well-positioned chests of drawers lined the walls. But it was the box now in the center of the floor between the sofas and the dark large desk that drew my attention. The box was now situated atop what bled through to be the insignia of a large bird of prey.

The room continued its three dimensional emergence with colors so florid they seemed to suggest emotions were in residence within inanimate objects. Then the people appeared in similar fashion, sitting opposite each other on the opposing sofas. A group of five were now assembled; men and women, to be sure, though their still and ghastly gray faces confused the distinction. None moved but remained as frozen as I'd observed the ashen-faced people in the great hall in my previous dreams. From this sprung the thought that these people situated on the sofas were merely an audience of some kind and not actual participants. The thought continued that I should re-examine the room for a source.

It was at that moment the sight of a single form registered. The form of a man with a malformed mind advanced in my awareness; one who maneuvered maniacal imaginings into public policy with the motions of his pen. A singularly sinister soul he harbored and I *knew* him. In the way a man knows his own evil intentions, I *knew* him.

His bowed head kept buoyed a thicket of disheveled hair. The mildly sloping shoulders of his tailored navy blue suit jacket jostled the minds of onlookers with their suggestions of superiority. His demeanor conveyed an air of masterliness, though over what or whom he exercised this mastery was not immediately discernible.

And still he continued writing, unaware of my dream-eye fixed upon him. I *knew* him. I couldn't shake that feeling. I understood him, or some part of him, and identified that part to be his insidious inflow to my essence. I despised him and his writing, whatever it was.

Something moved in the room and I motioned my dream-eye from the man and toward the detected disturbance. There, on the floor, fingers felt their way through and began folding the top flaps of the box inward. Strong, sturdy fingers, as one would attribute to a hulking male form, maneuvered the flaps silently and slowly, as though deceitfully, then braced themselves along the rim of the small box in preparation to pull its attached body into a world in which it did not belong.

I watched intently, noting that *I* seemed to be the only

entity aware of the strange occurrence in the room. The ashen-faced five on the sofa remained motionless and, in time, I regarded them as incapable of movement, for whatever reason that might be.

The body the adult male hands helped to emerge from the box was that of the child I'd interacted with in my first dream—the one who'd given me the box and the impression that it was I who was to have descended into it. Perhaps, then, it was I who should now be ascending from it. I focused on the child and the purposeful way it surveyed the room; its androgynous features again stirring some discomfort within me.

It moved, and in doing so, the salient sound of heavily clanking chains, though no chains were present, signaled an ominous occurrence. The child's height, though not tall, was prominent enough in front of the desk where it stood that its head should have been easily seen by the man sitting at the desk. However, there was no indication the child was detected by him or by the cadaverously pallid statues sitting on the sofas.

Amidst the jangling of invisible chains the child maneuvered around the large desk until it came to stand on the left side of the man seated there. So ensconced was he with his writing that he didn't appear to perceive the child. The child, however, could not be *known* in that room, I understood. *It* was not a true biological structure, but a Logos. *Its* existence in the room was the cause of the room's creation. *It* was the reason the room flowed into obedient being. *It* existed first, before the room's existence could be defined and came into the world *It* had created.

Near the left side of the man, the child still stood. My attempt to discern what, if any, meaning this placement represented yielded this: *Left* was the correct course for *me*—the course crafted by my Creator. I watched with my dream-eye, anticipating some singularly spectacular scene to play out and became agitated when the child raised its left hand in an attitude of instruction and gestured a violent stabbing motion into the man's neck. I then pulled away from my dream state, allowing my dream-eye to close, and awoke to find my shirt heavily-sodden with perspiration.

*   *   *

The hotel room seemed smaller than I had remembered it; as though the corners had somehow been drawn in while I slept and slowly continued to be while I was now awake. This was my impression as I sat on the bed—my back against the headboard. More importantly, I suspected the corners of the room to be malevolently dark. Though the room was smaller, the corners seemed resistant to the encroachment of light and the resident darkness there behaved, I thought, with hostility toward the bedside lamplight, pushing its luminescence back so aggressively I felt I could be harmed in the confrontation.

The room was dangerous, plain and simple. My returning unease reminded me of the publications I'd picked up in the convenience shop. On the bedside table they lay beside the obligatory digital hotel clock. I leaned over and collected them, noting the time in the process—5:13 a.m. I had not slept long. With my sleep-state tormented by sadistic dreams and my conscious self convinced of evil in every shadowy corner, I felt myself taxed by exhaustion and incapable of examining my dream with any clarity. I opened the publication of Brooklyn

apartments and scoured its scanty offerings, latching on
to a listing in the Flatbush section that seemed suitable in
price, but which held the unsavory distinction of being
a neighborhood densely populated by Afro-Caribbean
people. The reality was that I was a white man who, given
the present circumstances, did not want to stand out or to
be seen by anyone, or any *thing*.

The apartment was described as an *attic* apartment.
There was a private shower installed and a tiny make-shift
kitchen could be seen in the grainy photo. There were
windows on all sides and I wondered if this was a good
or bad circumstance for controlling the production of
shadows. I concluded that I would need to control the light
in the space and left off thinking about the matter. One
bright lamp placed in each of the corners would probably
accomplish this but I determined to let the theatrical
department at the university advise me. While there, I
could approach a friend I had who worked there, a fellow
poet who was also a screenwriter, and press him into
loaning me the needed fixtures.

There was, of course, the question of finances.
Specifically, how to afford the rent of five hundred dollars
per month the homeowners were asking, in addition to
the obligation I already had with my current apartment.
My accommodations in Brooklyn had to be short term, but
long enough until I found a way out of the mire I'd found
myself in. If no resolution could be found, then I could
never return home. Nor could I return to the university,
since my pursuer had an intimate knowledge of the place
and could wait there to catch me. No. A speedy resolution
was paramount. For the moment, however, sleep sought
me again and I welcomed it. The plan for my next steps
would have to wait until daylight. It had occurred to me

in my confused state that I was hiding from a shadow as though it was a single and individualized entity while simultaneously refraining from producing new shadows. But so little of present events was understood by me that I decided to avoid any shadow I might cast entirely.

I lay on my back and looked up at the ceiling through the darkness. A panicked blowfly could be heard buzzing in the room. Closing my eyes, I allowed myself to enter a new darkened space and there found a peace that ensconced me. I surrendered to it, welcoming its caresses. For the moment, fear had left me and I drifted off without dread or tumult.

*　　*　　*

The late morning sun, together with the tentative tapping by a member of the hotel's housekeeping staff, carried me to consciousness. I did not feel rested. The first few moments after my waking found me confused and not knowing where I was, or the events that brought me there. After a few seconds, the fog dissipated and I quickly dismissed the employee before she could enter the room. The bedside clock revealed 10:42 AM and I called down to the front desk to see if a noon check-out was possible. They agreed and I promptly entered the bathroom to shower.

The question of the fallen tree and whether it is dead the moment it is felled, or still alive when felled but beginning the slow process of death—this question returned while I showered, and it occupied my thoughts for the remainder of my time at the hotel. It seemed to me, and I concluded, that the question was unanswerable until I understood, precisely, what death was. On its face, the question of death's definition seemed nonsensical and unnecessary. Death was the cessation of life, most would say. But this answer seemed cheap and dismissive. There was more to this question that invited exploration, and I promised myself, as I closed the room door behind me, to revisit these thoughts at a later time.

*   *   *

The homeowners met me at the taxi. It was a charming, old-world thing to do and it warmed my spirits. As I emerged from the cab, the dingy white frame house stood behind them against a cloudy sky. The upper floors contrasted bitterly against the gathering gray storm clouds and filled me with terror. Death donned a disguise for me here. Also, I felt that I'd been there before. But, it was all no matter, I reasoned within. Death, whatever it was, waited for me at all turns if I could not get my present situation in hand. There was no escaping this reality. I inspected the apartment with the homeowners and found it a habitable hide-out. Notwithstanding the three large cockroaches I spied entering a separation where the wall and ceiling met on the apartment's south side, I agreed to rent the place, but only if my tenancy could begin immediately. The homeowners watched me as I conspicuously eyed the roaches and accepted my request without delay. The limits on the wattage of the bulbs I would use in my fixtures (I told them I was a writer and theatrical production student) and the closing of the blinds were the only caveats they required. But these I have already mentioned. I gave them the bills I'd taken from

the bank on my way over to them, five hundred dollars
in total, received the keys and then left for the university
to obtain the light fixtures. I felt reasonably sure that my
pursuer would not stake out the theatrical department
since that department was located in a building I rarely
entered and of which It had little knowledge of. My plans
were shaping up and I took some comfort in the sense of
forward momentum.

*   *   *

On my return trip from the university, I detoured to a
rustic Army and Navy supply store on the neighborhood's
Flatbush Avenue that I'd noticed during my earlier
taxi ride in to see the homeowners. There I purchased a
sleeping bag, a flashlight and a folding pocket knife I knew
would be useless against my pursuer. I felt safer having it,
nonetheless. Such is the wiring that comprises the human
primate. I also purchased two cases of bottled water, but I
determined hunger would need to be satisfied by whatever
home delivery options existed. The light fixtures, I was
told, would be delivered the following evening, when the
theatrical department's van and driver were next available.
This concluded the day's preparations. Freshly fatigued, I
returned to my hideout to settle in and to consider my next
steps.

*   *   *

The fluorescent bulbs hummed and crackled under
the strain to deliver what was to become the blinding,
intolerable light. Somewhere in the house, someone, a

56

ᶃ some silly song. The song saddened
ᴜ the emotion caused me to question
ᴤss of freedom, if its requisite attendant was
ᴤs.

ᴧay on my sleeping bag, partially nude, using my
ᴧded pants under the rear of my head as a pillow. When
I'd last looked out the window approximately twenty
minutes prior, I'd noted the season and the waning
sunlight above the clouds and approximated the time to be
not much past seven in the evening. I'd closed the blinds
to the windows at that time, turned on the lamps I've
previously described and satisfied myself that no shadows
were being borne by me in the bare space.

I, again, pondered my dreams on this, my second night;
turning them around repeatedly in my mind, pulling them
apart to examine their constituent components, moving
them closer then further away in trombonic fashion to
note and comprehend their complexion and complexity,
trying to find some modicum of sense or similarity in the
seemingly disassociated dissections. I was a madman; a
man without self-knowledge or a dark side upon which
he could cast his evil imaginings and so wore them on his
person as a miner dons the dirt produced by his labor on
his face. I felt myself becoming—and more frighteningly
still—*appearing* to become a monster; a form of Dorian
Gray's picture that no man should see, but which every
man would see, in time.

The motionless ashen-gray people were of concern to
me. Who were they? What did they represent? They were
always positioned in my dreams so that they might see or
bear witness, yet I could not reasonably conclude that they
had ever *seen* anything.

The box that was given to me and which I now

understood was mine to descend into also drew concern. What did it represent? Why did it have precise measurements? Was my anticipated descent into it a representation of my descent into an underworld? Or, perhaps, into madness?

I turned these thoughts and questions around in my mind. However, the most disturbing recurrence was the child—if I dared call it that—and its interest in me. Or, its message for me. This *being* I found myself reluctant to parse in my analysis of my dreams. There was something too terrifying in that entity and, as a result, I could not comfortably approach it, even in my investigative thoughts.

Worse than these dream-things were the events perforating my reality. I was a man pursued by a malevolent force I did not understand. I'd contemplated the idea of him and believed I'd extrapolated certain things from our limited interactions. Unsure whether my apprehensions were sound or mere transferences of my notions onto the entity, I noted there existed a child-like quality in this being; an underdeveloped personage, in some respects testing and teasing my mind, observing me, contemplating me, pursuing me.

The thought that this entity, even now, perhaps, was waiting in my apartment for my return caused me to shudder. What was its connection to all this? Was there a connection at all? To these questions and all the others preceding them, no answers presented themselves. I concluded that a plan of action was what was needed. And that plan had to begin with engaging the shadow, since it, alone, presented itself in reality and not in dreams.

But how does one engage the unknown? By throwing one's self headfirst into the abyss? This was the only way.

child perhaps, sang some silly song. The song saddened me, I noted, and the emotion caused me to question the usefulness of freedom, if its requisite attendant was loneliness.

Just as the darkness in the corners of my hotel room pushed back the light in order to reach me, so, too, was the darkness in the abyss reaching up to devour me where I stood. There was no escaping it. And though I'd like to report that all fear left me at that moment, as I lay on my sleeping bag grasping this new realization, it did not. The fear remained—but with a more simple complexity.

I switched off the lamps without knowing the time and returned to lie on top of the sleeping bag. The sawing sound of a panicked blowfly betrayed the room's calm. I shut out the sound from my consciousness and focused on my pursuer and how I might engage him. I'm unsure how long I persisted in that mental pursuit, but before long I detected a heaviness above the eyes and a *sinking* in my belly. Then another place came to be, and I drifted off to it.

*   *   *

The room was as I remembered it—just as I'd left it. The lamp on the bedside table continued to shine, the brightness from that beacon persisting in its struggle to press back the darkness. The bed I sat on with my back against its headboard felt the same. And the obligatory digital hotel clock beside the lamp read "13:9:8"—an unintelligible time, to be sure, but I understood its import in some other area of my consciousness.

The light, as I observed it, fought bravely and brought the room closer to proper proportions during the periods it prevailed against the darkness. At those times a box on the floor was illuminated in the opposite left corner of the room. When the darkness prevailed against the light, the room contracted, drawing closer to me. The box then

59

disappeared from view, having lost its illuminating source.

I got up and stood alongside the bed contemplating the arrival of the box and its seeming undulations between this world and some other. My behavior here alerted me that something had changed about me since I had never before understood my dream-self to actually contemplate *anything*. In fact, until that point, I was convinced that dream characters did not think, but simply observed and felt. They reacted to their observations and feelings in much the same way base animals do, without contemplation.

Retrieving the box from the corner was now my mind's occupation, but the ebb and flow of the darkness posed a challenge. I did not want to be touched by *that* darkness. Near me, however, a solution presented itself and, turning to it, I grabbed the bedside lamp by its trunk and held it as a sword against the room's corner so that the lamplight flowed unfiltered through the top of the lampshade. The darkness retreated with a sigh analogous to those of dying men. I heard it plainly.

I nudged the box, with its closed flaps, from the corner with my left foot. The vague notion went through me of reserving the use of the lamp as a weapon, should something unexpected emerge from the box's enclosure. Once the box was near the bed, I returned the lamp to the night table, tilted its shade to cast more light on the box and then studied the thing a long moment. It was just as I'd remembered it, when the child gave it to me in the great hall, before I'd removed the sun from it.

The odd time on the clock's display had not changed: "13:9:8". Kneeling over the box, I unfolded the flaps and peered in. Only darkness greeted me; a darkness not dispelled by the lamplight shining into it; a bottomless abyss. The same as I'd expected. The same as I'd feared.

With trepidation I put my left foot in the box, and then my right, purposefully not intending to stop my descent into the thing no matter what tentacle of terror seized me. To explain my ability to fit in the box and to describe my means of descent would be as perplexing as its meaning would be unintelligible. Suffice it to say that I fit into the box because I willed it and descended because I purposed to.

The descent was brief and inexplicable, in that it was unlike moving down a ladder, staircase or by elevator. However, the act of descending was actual and real. I did this in the impenetrable darkness, until the sense that I was descending ceased...and the sense that I was alone settled in.

My left hand felt a foreign palm slip into it. From the angle of its grasp, I assumed a child had taken me. But the hand was much larger than a child's, and quite coarse. My instinct to recoil was checked by the realization that if I were to disengage from this hand, I would be left without a guide through this blackness, as well as a potential enemy in the form of an unknown entity. Retreating or ascending was not possible, since I did not possess an intuition as to how to achieve it. So, I complied with the tugging hand and allowed myself to be led—transported by some strange motion through the darkness.

The only way I can describe it is that we *moved*. I can make no representation of the speed in which we travelled. The unbounded darkness was so complete and devoid of properties such as air, wind, or even scent, that moving through it was an immeasurable event. I can say, though, that we didn't seem to be moving for any extreme length of time before we came across a rectangular outline of thin yellow light appearing vertically in front of us. I understood it immediately to be a door of some sort, and the light framing it to be that from a room beyond. The hand released mine and I gave no further thought to the entity's existence in the space.

*

The apartment was just as I'd remembered it—now that I'd stepped through the doorway and into this new space. The TV was still okay. Wasn't broken or nothing. Seeing it, though, made it real what I was feeling. And what I was feeling was that I was part of some disruption in time and space. Kinda like I'd been here before, but also like I hadn't. Hard to really explain it.

Moving around the room, I let myself pass over things that were supposed to be important. Books on bookshelves, handwritten papers on a table. Stuff like that. None of it was really interesting. And none of it really had anything to do with me. But I was probably a part of it all somehow. Whatever. I don't really have anything to say about it. It'll be what it is. *Stupid*.

I circled the place a few times then came up near the back of the sofa. He was lying there on his back, with his right arm stretched out off the side and laying on the coffee table next to a bottle. I looked at him a long time. A long time. Then I moved around the front of the sofa and stood against the wall, studying him again from a different angle. Resting my hands on my hips, I looked at him a long time. A long long time trying to figure out what I wanted to do. One thing was sure: I didn't like him.

I didn't like his thoughts. I didn't like the way he

talked. His dreams were disgusting to me and stupid. Stupid poetry. How far did he think he would get with that? What was he trying to *do*, anyway? Who was he trying to *be*? His arguments didn't even make sense to me. I didn't understand them. I looked at him a long time from his stupid feet all the way to his stupid face. I hid in the shadows when I realized he had been staring back at me.

"Don't. Don't. Or, I'll kill you. I will kill you where you stand." The fool had stood up and kept looking in a panicked way at the light switch by the apartment door. The coward. I'd always suspected as much. But here it was. "Do you know who I am?" I asked him.

"No."

"Do you know *what* I am?"

"No." he answered, more slowly this time.

"I see. You should sit. There's something I want to tell you." He sat, but in a way that made me feel his intention was to run at the first opportunity. I repeated my warning to him.

"I understand. I won't do anything unless you tell me to," the coward rambled on. "Who are you? What do you want? Have I harmed you in some way? If so, I'm sorry. How did you get into my apartment?"

"I know you," I answered. "You're a fraud. You're part of a problematic group of delusional fraudsters. I've been following your movements for a while now. Do you think you're some kind of god? Or, some kind of mythical creature with the *preeminent light of understanding*? I bet you'd like it if I called you 'Your Eminence'. Alright, then. 'Your Eminence the Fraudster' it is."

I paused and watched him from the darkness. I knew him. I was right about that. But he knew nothing about me at all. I don't know why, but at that moment I began to wonder if I knew *myself*. Watching him from the darkness, I felt, at that moment, that I could be dangerous. That he was making me dangerous.

"You can call me whatever you wish," he replied. "Even though you mock me, I will answer you. 'Your Eminence' is fine."

"I will not call you 'Your Eminence.'"

"Well. It was *your* suggestion," he continued.

I despised him. I knew him and I despised him. His stupid face was looking in my direction from the sofa. I wanted to smash it. The fool. Passing from cowardice to cunning without understanding anything. Stupid and arrogant. By now he had to have been making a plan. A moronic plan, no doubt. But a plan he thought was clever. But he didn't know me. And I had something planned for *him*.

"Never mind that, Fraudster."

"And what should I call *you*?"

"It doesn't matter. It's only the two of us here. If you start talking, you're obviously talking to *me*. No need to call my attention."

"Not necessarily," he replied. "I could be speaking to myself. I *am* prone to doing that."

"You're stupid." I repeated. "But never mind that. You think I'm an intruder. Why would I give you any part of my name?"

"I simply thought that since we were speaking as gentlemen that we'd follow convention and trade names. I haven't called you an intruder, have I? I am Per. Initials would suffice given the circumstances. Mine are P.I."

I kept watching him from the shadows. I wanted to harm him the way I felt he had harmed me. I thought about it and couldn't really say *how* he'd harmed me. But

I knew he had. Was he harming me now? Is this how he does it? I played along and gave him a piece of myself—with a twist.

"i.d.," I told him. "In the lower case if you please."

"I see. Very well," he paused. "But I'm sorry. I don't know how to speak in lower case. Is that what you mean?"

"Yes. I know you don't. That's part of your problem." Talking to him was beginning to bother me. "You can call me whatever you want. I will answer you."

"Oh. Again, very well. How long will you ride this carousel?"

I watched him from the shadows. I watched him as he got angry. He continued speaking.

"I was under the impression that you'd come to harm me. Now I see you've come to either tickle my sides or to annoy me."

"You're a fool," I started. "And now...". But just as I started talking, I felt myself being pulled away—dissolving—from that place. I'm not sure if I'd even finished my sentence; whatever it was I was intending to say.

*

I witnessed myself, in the first person, stepping backwards out of the box. As inconsequential as the knowledge felt to me at the time, I noted that I wasn't led through the darkness or guided in my ascension. In fact, there was no darkness or ascension as a part of my return. I merely stepped backwards out of the box.

The hotel room seemed different, and I understood it to be an *in-between* place. The space still appeared as I remembered it, in that everything was in its proper place, but the color to the room had somehow withdrawn. The hue to the space had become dull as if the thing had been "used up". I felt unsure whether or not I could ever return to it.

After folding the box flaps closed I placed the thing under my left arm. A glance at the bedside clock revealed nothing. The object had gone dark.

*

I awoke at what I perceived to be the small hours of the morning, amidst the distinct sound of whispers in the room. I was cold and heavily-sodden with sweat. The portion of my sleeping bag I had been lying on was drenched, particularly where my torso had lain. The whispering seemed to come from everywhere. I was surrounded by it, but felt no fear.

Having stood up, I stepped carefully through the dark and turned on the first of the floor lamps. The whispers retreated from that corner of the room. I noted this and repeated my action with the remaining three lamps in their respective corners. The whispers vanished entirely from the space. An odd occurrence, but I put no thought into it, instead telling myself that I was either still dreaming or in some way insufficiently awake. I flipped my sleeping bag over to access its dry side, then proceeded to turn the lamps off and to feel with my feet my way back to my slumbering place. The whispers did not return with the renewed darkness and as indecipherable as they had been, no curiosity welled inside me as to what they were trying to communicate. I simply closed my eyes and let the episode pass.

*

I awoke again at what I perceived to be the mid-morning hours, to the expressive sound of humming opposite the door to my room. A pale early-morning light filtered through the drawn blinds and I imagined the time to be somewhere around 7 or 8 AM. The humming was, in its own way, similar to the singing I'd heard the evening of my arrival—and I suspected the child had made its way to the top of the stairs with a boredom-induced curiosity. I put on my clothes and opened the door for a look.

The child sat on the top step of the staircase, with her left side nearest to me. On the landing beside her were three halved clam shells that appeared to have been painted with the glitter-infused nail polish that pre-teen girls were often fond of. *This* child, however, couldn't have been older than seven-years-old. She was slender—slight, even—with black shoulder-length hair, and with features and a complexion reminiscent of India. She was an extraordinarily pretty child, and I stared at her a moment before prudently reorienting myself to reality.

"Hi," she started without looking at me. She'd turned slightly, only to pick up and fondle the clam shells. I could tell her other senses were trained intently on me.

"Hi," I replied, with a smile intended to be disarming. "What's your name?"

"Saraswati. Everybody calls me Sara." She looked at her shells admiringly, turning them over and over in her hands. "I heard you talking in your sleep."

I chuckled a bit. "Really? But I don't talk in my sleep."

"How do you know?"

"Well," I started, then pausing to search for an appropriate answer. "I've never been told that I do."

"But *I've* just told you." She raised her left eyebrow in a way one might expect an adult to. "Anyway, it was just a lot of whispering. I knew you were alone so I figured you were sleep-talking. It woke me up."

I remained silent. I did recall the whispers but was quite certain I did not produce them. She continued speaking but still did not look at me.

"Do you think it matters?"

"*What* does?"

"The tree," she replied. "Do you think it matters if it's dead or dying? Once it's cut off from its Source, life is no longer possible."

I was dumbfounded. Both by the simplistic wisdom in her analysis as well as by the path our conversation now took.

"Is that what you heard me whispering in my sleep?"

"Yes." She put the shells down beside her on the landing and looked at them. "But you shouldn't be afraid. I think only people who are fearful would split hairs on the subject of death."

She wrapped her fingers tightly around the shells and then stood abruptly, readying herself to descend the stairs. My pride, stung by her words, made an attempt at redemption. I quickly spoke before she started down the steps, and I no longer displayed a smile.

"What makes you think I'm afraid? Or fearful? It doesn't necessarily follow that because I posit a philosophical question about death that I'm fearful of dying."

She looked at me for the first time. Her eyes were as

black as jet stone.

"Was the tree question a *philosophical* one?" She paused a second then placed her left foot on the step below her while smiling up at me. "You're not the first person to come here with a sleeping bag from a taxi."

She descended out of sight. The space felt barren with her absence. I closed the door and retreated to my sleeping bag, where I sat and pondered her words. It was my third day there and high time I arose from this slumbering other world of shadows, fear and hiding. Sara was right. It was also the case that, though I'd showered the prior day, I still wore the same clothing I had left my apartment wearing. I decided to go home—to pick up my bed and walk. I decided to leave this place, return the lamps to the university and go home. I could no longer continue as one separated from his Source.

*　　*　　*

And I entered my apartment which seemed a singularly distant place from how I recalled it. "Distant" in the sense that the space felt as though my absence had been three years and not the three days that had passed. Exhausted from my scurrying all over town, organizing the return of the lamps to the university, I still remained aware—cautious, even—of the space I'd entered. Sara's words remained with me, however, and I did not fear.

After entering, I placed my rolled sleeping bag on the floor next to the door and stood a moment searching the space with all available senses. It wasn't long, however, before I noticed a shadow contrasting darkly on the same wall where I'd noticed it for the first time a few days prior—with its arms akimbo in similar fashion. I moved instinctively to the opposite side of the room and turned to face it directly. This time, it did not seek to hide. Its intent was to engage and I chose to do the same—though I had no idea how.

"You're here," I heard the thing say in the same threateningly calm voice I remembered of it.

"Yes."

"I felt you. I knew you were here." It lowered its arms from its hips. "I've been looking for you."

"I'm here. We've found each other."

"Well, let's begin then." As it spoke, it seemed to me that its form transmogrified before my very eyes.

In confusion, I watched, not grasping this strange occurrence. Then, in a moment of clarity, I understood. The thing was changing. It was moving itself from a two-dimensional figure against the wall to a three-dimensional figure occupying space in the room. Its movement while doing so was slow, and I got the sense there was labor involved in the shift. But after it separated from the wall and stood in front of it, its presence was striking and dreadful, though not as dark as it had been before the transformation. It had lost a bit of its essence in the shift and was a paler representation of its two-dimensional self.

"Oh, Jesus!" I heard myself exclaim. "What do you want from me?!" So disturbing was the sight of *him* that I felt myself begin convulsing toward a panic.

"Your neck."

Here he postured as though to lunge at me from across the room. Only the length of the sofa lay between us.

"Wait! *Wait!*" But it did not wait. In a flash he was upon me; his shadowy arms flailing while his hands grasped at my neck whenever they were able to evade my defensive maneuvers. There were moments when my bare neck was touched by *it* and in those moments a cold and clammy sensation was felt, along with pressure against my throat. But strangely, whenever I knocked away his hands I did not register contact with an object containing mass. In other words, I could not feel myself striking the *thing*, but my striking it was still with effect.

"Hold still, you rat," I heard *him* mutter. "Be dead for a due cat."

"Wait! Wait! Stop!" I again yelled out. Here a chance moment presented itself through the flurry of harassing hands, and I was able to dart to the right of *him* and escape. I sensed my shirt at the right shoulder break free from a final clutch. "I know the problem! I know the problem! Wait!"

And there I stood. And there *it* stood, approximately thirteen feet away from me and opposite the sofa. Though it had no face for me to judge an expression, I held the distinct impression his state was either one of confusion or interest. It spoke.

"You know... the *problem?*"

"Yes! Yes! It's in what you said." I tried to control my panic. It was interfering with my breathing. "Let me explain."

It did not respond here. And it did not move. I took the inactivity to mean it was waiting for my explanation or was halted by indecision. I seized the blankness and continued.

"It's what you said: 'A rat, dead for a ducat'." I gasped for air. "It's what Hamlet says when he killed Polonius who he thought was the king hiding behind a curtain. Don't you see? The problem is the king. Or, rather, the leader. Or *government*. Or whatever you want to call it."

"Your lying neck. You're trying to trick me. That's why you've come back. So *this* is how you do it."

"No! I swear to you. Think about it." I paused here a few seconds to review my thoughts. No doubt the move made them seem more authentic and not premeditated. "This all started when I began writing the poem, didn't it? A few nights ago. And what was the poem about? Government! The leader, Washington, D.C., and the dissolution of morality and civility! Don't you see?! Was it *you* who tried to stop me?"

It didn't answer straight away, but began pacing its side of the room, its shadowy essence gradually fading as it did. "Hmm. I *do* see," it said finally. "I *do* remember. This is no trick."

I continued to watch him but did nothing to rouse him from thought. I remained silent and marked his continual fading, wondering if he would discover it and what, if anything, would happen if he did not. Then it occurred to me: It was a thing cut off from its source.

"Yes, Yes. I see," he resumed, still pacing. "Something must be done." He stopped and turned his "body" to face me. He placed his hands on his hips. "What do you think?"

"*Absolutely,* something must be done," I answered. "The circles of our lives need not be deformed by the depressions of government. I can't let that happen."

It stood there, facing me, for a short while that felt laboriously lengthy. I was unsure what to make of the pause. But I knew from his question to me that something fundamental had shifted in his attitude toward me. I didn't speak, but I got the sense *he* wanted me to.

"Yes, but," he spoke tentatively, "What will you *do?*"

"*I?*" I repeated with emphasis. "*I* can do nothing. I am a victim of the leader and its government, which controls even my very thoughts and desires; as we saw with the poem that started all this. Even my interests stand in opposition to me."

It did not respond to this. I noted in the present silence how his last question confirmed the notion I'd had some time ago about him. He was, indeed, child-like. The timid, direction-seeking way he delivered his last question was a perfect exemplar of that quality. I continued speaking to it to advance the present direction of things.

"But *we*. *We* can do something, perhaps. What do *you* think we should do?"

"Kill him."

"Kill the leader?"

"Yes."

"But," I measured my words here. A strategy for my thoughts lagged. The response he gave had not been expected. "What about the government he leads? What shall we do about *it?*"

"If you choke the head the body will die, won't it?"

"Conceptually, yes."

"Then we kill the body by choking it off from its source, the head."

Perplexed to hear him use the words "its source", I wondered why he chose them and why he would use them *now*. I did not recall having a conversation with him in which I intimated my thoughts about the tree. Nevertheless, I found it satisfying to hear him attempt to thrash out the complexities of things I'd ruminated over, regardless of how he happened to come across them—or however wrong his conclusions were.

"It's not that simple. America is a democracy and, as

such, the power is concentrated in the head but doesn't reside there. The head is not the source of the power. The power resides in the body. If you kill the head, a new one will grow."

"Then we kill the body and the head will die. Either way we must choke it. It doesn't matter which dies first."

"No," I reasoned, suppressing a sigh. "That won't work either. It seems when you attack the body, the head becomes stronger."

I stopped talking here, not knowing where the conversation was headed and feeling foul at hearing the words I spoke. All I longed for was to sleep. It was as if a fresh wave of exhaustion flooded over me. At that moment, the shadow lifted its arms and seemed, by the movement of its head, to examine them from hand to shoulder. It then examined its torso and body and, I gathered, realized it was fading.

"Okay," it replied while repositioning its head to face me. "You sleep on it. You sleep on it and I'll try to figure it out."

And on completing this statement he moved back to the wall he'd originated from and once again became the two-dimensional figure I'd previously known him to be. For my part, I moved to the sofa and lay there on my back and in the position that allowed me to view the wall he'd gone to. I was desperately tired as a result of not receiving restful sleep these past few days. But now, it was as if something lost had been restored to me and that the sleep I would now receive would be satisfying. As my eyes closed I looked at the shadow on the wall in the early moonlight and noticed it had taken a sitting position in profile. With an elbow on its knee and its chin on its hand, it resembled the Rodin bronze sculpture, *The Thinker*. I smiled at this and then shut my thoughts away from my drifting consciousness.

*   *   *

The room was as I remembered it—but not as I'd left it. The fluorescent bulbs hummed and crackled under the strain to deliver their once-blinding and intolerable light. I remembered them now, in this place. Their light, once white, energetic and transformative, now took on an aggressively dark hue that pulsated between the walls like breathing. It was a remarkable sight. Without losing their intensity, the lights seemed as though they shone from a distant and malevolent world, far removed from where I stood. However, remarkable as it appeared, I understood this to be a dangerous place—dangerous in that this manifestation of the room was an *in-between* place, as I'd come to know them.

I stood over the sleeping bag, contemplating the arrival of the box and its deliberate placement on the bag, in the area where my head would have rested. Its flaps were closed but even so, diminutive whispers could be heard from its enclosure. I stood there over the box in benign contemplation, but knowing what my involvement with it had to be.

Crouching, I grasped the thing and moved it off the bag and onto the hardwood floor near it. I then unfolded the flaps and peered inside. The expected impenetrable darkness greeted me while the whispers became markedly louder. Strangely, though the volume of the whispers increased, the words in the whispers were no less indecipherable. Loud, wordless whispers filled that peculiar place and held me for a time, through an intimacy embedded in its current. I did not know what the whispers were saying, but somehow knew what they sought.

Without trepidation, I put my left foot in the box and then my right. I *purposed* to descend and by so doing experienced a descent that was brief and inexplicable in that it was unlike moving down a ladder, staircase or by elevator. However, the act of descending was actual and real.

My left hand felt a familiar palm slip into it. I complied with its tugging and was led, transported by a strangely familiar motion, through the darkness. It was an immeasurable event. But in time, the hand released mine and I witnessed myself, in the first person, stepping backwards out of the box.

*

The hotel room was how I had last seen it. Its dull hue still appeared as though its existence had been "used up". Though I was previously unsure whether I could ever return to this *in-between* place, I apparently did. A pivot of my head to the left revealed the bedside clock—still dark. No odd numbers showed on the display. A continued pivot of my head further to the left revealed a new enclosure in the space. This *enclosure* was a being; ashen in its entirety from head to foot and as motionless as the statue-like figures I'd recalled from previous dreams. This being, however, stood beside the bedside table and faced the expanse of the room. It held a box under its left arm, and I understood at that moment that the being was *me,* or some altered version of myself; dull and used-up.

I looked again at the box I'd just stepped from, but did not pick it up. Crouching, I closed the flaps, then stood again and moved the thing with my left foot to the shadowy corner of the room near me. Once there, the thing left my consciousness and I could no longer see it. From there, I passed softly by the ashen being and sat on the bed, placing my back against the headboard and stretching my legs out before me. Peculiar periods of time passed before I became conscious again of a box in the shadowy corner opposite the bed. Without understanding how I knew this, the knowledge that the box was a different *structure* from the one I'd placed there earlier was apparent. I got off the bed, moved over to the thing and nudged it from the corner with my left foot. Then, crouching once again, I opened the flaps and observed the darkness within.

My descent was as previous descents had been, and by now, was an unremarkable journey for me. The hand that tugged mine and the awkward sense of motionless movement were similarly customary. However, the vertically-placed rectangle I now stood before was different from the last. Whereas the previous rectangle I'd encountered was formed of a thin, yellow light, this one was a deep crimson, resembling blood. The inflow to my being while standing before the crimson frame was that such frames were rare, and that an unbalanced evil resided beyond. I understood the inflow to mean that crimson around a doorframe was a mark signaling that only a balancing entity—a *negating* evil or corrective angel—should venture beyond. I understood the inflow infallibly and drew confirmation of its import when the once-tugging hand slipped from mine.

*

The room had good lighting and was familiar, like I'd been there before. I don't know why, since nothing in the place had anything to do with me. But, whatever. I stood against the wall and noticed right away that it had a strange shape; like an egg, it was oval in the way it outlined the room. I didn't like this. It was stupid. Right angles were better, I felt. In normally-shaped rooms, if light from the windows was all you had, you could count on at least one or maybe even two walls being in the shadows. Shadowy walls were good hiding places. But *this* room was different. It was oval. And if that didn't make things hard enough for me, the place in the room where I needed to go—a large desk on the other side of two big sofas—didn't have a normal wall. Behind the desk were all large windows with daylight coming through them. There wasn't a way for me to crawl, unseen, against the wall and sneak up behind the chair at the desk. The designers of the room seemed to plan the room against visitors like me. But I had my trick.

I stopped thinking about the room's navigational problems and started looking to see what other *entities* might be there to stop me. On the other side of the room, sitting at his great big desk, with his head bowed down while writing something, was the problem I'd come to sort out. He was stupid for not looking up to see me; stupid for not feeling my presence in the room. I didn't like him. Everything about him, and the way he behaved with his stupid writing annoyed me.

The two sofas were facing each other and were between me and the desk at the other end of the oval. On them these dark gray statue-people were sitting. Their heads faced the desk where the man sat writing—but they didn't look alive. The feeling returned, that I'd been there once before. The statue-people made me feel that. But I wasn't concerned about them and blocked them from my purpose. Seeing my path, I crouched down and took it.

Across the floor I moved, slowly; as slowly as the shadow of a cloud might move across the floor of a big room with big windows on a partly-sunny day. No one would have spotted me, even if there was an entity in the room that could. Slowly I moved. That was the way. Slowly. When death comes slowly, no one notices. I'd learned this. Aging is a slow death, but nobody fears aging. Nations die slowly from within, but there are no calls to arms. I'd learned this, too. But from where, I couldn't say.

Time passed. And I eventually came across a box in the middle of the room, close to the great big desk. I remembered this box from somewhere, though it was out of place where it was. Somebody left it there in the middle of the floor, sitting on top of a large bird of prey design that was part of the carpet. I had been in this room before, though I couldn't say how or when. I just knew. Slowly, I moved past the box and reached the base of the great big desk.

And here I rose to my feet, standing tall and full as a man before the great big desk—transitioning to energy and being as full of life as my trick allowed me. I felt strong and his neck was only seconds away from my hands. I was invigorated, as though I'd already completed my mission. But he didn't look up to see me. He scribbled away, with his head turned downward. I thought to read what he was writing from my upside-down position and felt myself fade a bit when his words flowed into my being:

"And so it is, as we've always said. Once the affected masses can no longer think critically, or think for themselves, they will group together, drawn by their shared identity, and shout empty slogans and craft silly placards based on erroneous data our fore-bearers have planted. These affected masses will argue and debate with presuppositions hand-picked by us. And we will listen. We must listen. For in our listening we appease them while learning where to further enslave them. To co-opt their politics of identity so that they love us..."

I stopped reading and let out a low growl. The man lifted his head and looked at me but kept on writing as he did this. His face was a normal face, except he had no eyes. Dark empty sockets faced me. His kept writing as he spoke.

"Who are you?"

"I am Ingenting Dröm."

"Why have you come?" His voice was slow and deep, but easily understood.

"To kill the head so that the body will die."

"I am the head. I am the body. I define you. I am all."

"Yes," I answered, feeling a small tremor begin under my feet as I spoke. "You are all."

I threw myself at him across the great big desk and put his throat in both hands. He didn't struggle. But the dark empty sockets, now closer to me than they had been, seemed to have *entities* in them; entities bent on escape. I squeezed his throat harder and let the exhilaration of the act pass through me.

He was dead before I even realized he was dead. The tremor I'd felt just a few seconds earlier was now growing into a rumbling. The room was shaking. The statue-people sitting on the sofas had at some point started laughing a high-pitched, cackling laughter. I let the throat go, stood again in front of the desk and looked around me, trying to understand why there was now a quaking in the room. The place was about to fall apart.

Turning, I looked to leave the room the same way I had come in—but this wasn't possible. The quaking was too severe, and I also understood that that doorway was forever closed. Looking at this being once more, I noticed that even though he was dead, he still sat upright in his chair. Dark liquid streamed from the empty eye sockets. I felt myself fading. *Fading.*

It was here I noticed the large hand pushing slowly through the top of the box, unfolding the flaps outward as it moved. Its slow motion didn't match the quaking of the room and the cackling laughter of the statue-people. I moved a few steps closer to the box and stood over it. The hand disappeared back into the box, and I placed my left foot into the welcoming darkness, and then my right. I went down into the thing, and the oval room no longer surrounded me.

*

I witnessed myself, in the first person, stepping backwards out of the box. I noted that I wasn't led through the darkness or guided in my ascension. There was no darkness or ascension as part of my return.

The hotel room did not seem different upon my re-emergence and I continued in my understanding that it was an *in-between* place. The room's colors remained

81

pallid; its hues still dull, as if the thing had been "used up".
I was certain that I could never return to it.

After folding the box flaps closed, I placed the thing
under my left arm. A slight trembling could be felt
underfoot, a distinct and approaching tremor could be felt
in the space. The bedside clock conveyed nothing. The
object remained dark. A further glance to the left revealed
my ashen and statue-like self holding its box, as I now held
mine. Its gaze continued across the room into nothingness.
I followed it and also turned my gaze to the room's
expanse. I turned my gaze toward the nothingness.

*

I witnessed myself, in the first person, stepping
backwards out of the box. I noted that I wasn't led through
the darkness or guided in my ascension. There was no
darkness or ascension as part of my return. I merely
stepped backwards out of the box.

The room was not as I remembered it and I continued
in my understanding that it was an *in between* place. The
color to the space was withdrawn; the hue to the space was
dull as if the thing had been "used up". I was certain that I
could never return to it.

I stood over the box and observed the sleeping bag and
its placement neatly alongside the box on the hardwood
floor. A shimmy to the place could be felt underfoot. An
approaching tremor could be felt in the space. In time this
place would collapse and be no more. After folding the
box flaps closed, I placed the thing under my left arm and
let my gaze drift towards the direction of the approaching
tremor. I let my gaze drift towards the nothingness.

*   *   *

The glow of a maturing morning filled the room.
Upon my awakening, I was lost in it and didn't
immediately know where I was, though the feeling that
my life had come full-circle was satisfying to me. I felt
rested and complete and surveyed the room from where I
lay on the sofa trying to reconstitute a continuity with the
previous day's events.

Sitting up on the sofa, I happened to glance at
my rolled sleeping bag on the floor by the door and
remembered Sara. A wise young soul she was, and
replaying her words in my mind allowed me to better
understand the new morning and my rejuvenated self.
The Source—the entity that creates, sustains and connects
all living things to Itself and to all other living things, had
reoriented me to Its truth. This was the wholeness I felt;
the peace I enjoyed at that moment. My circle no longer
contained a separation and I was complete.

In this spirit of *completion*, I rose to my feet, ascending
from my sleeping place and into a new realization
prepared just for me, it seemed. There is no "self," and
yet there are many "selves". Unnatural things exist, but
they are temporary. The universe will cause all things to
balance. Live wisely and in truth. Trust the Source.

I stepped from my apartment and let the cool air of
the corridor dry the water I'd splashed on my face. My
sense of motion was heightened by this baptism into a new
life. The sidewalk met me there and I travelled it alone.
Then, silently, the simultaneous steps of my wholeness
joined. Slipping beneath me in full circle, it joined—its

movements met mine as wings meet the wind.
    "There is no life without the Source," I said.
    "I am nothing but a dream."

The Store

The corner grocery store I was eyeing from my living room window was deteriorating rather quickly, I thought. Every day since its appearance across the street last fall, I had noticed, with marked consternation, some new blemish on the parchment of its existence. The green cloth canopy that was its crown and glory when it was new was today magnificently soiled with vertical white and gray streaks that the neighborhood pigeons, in their discerning way, had left as testament to the store's rapidly dilapidating character. The collection of streaks and pilings appeared years in the making, but I was certain it was not present when I observed the place last evening.

I also noticed, today, that the large shop windows that served the establishment had become filthy, literally overnight. From my window, it was no longer possible to see through them, though in truth, owing to the difference in height of the buildings and the distance of my flat from the store, I had never been able to see much in there. It was odd. The entire affair was odd—odd because as far as my memory served, I had never witnessed anyone enter or exit the place. I had never seen or heard the owners, whoever they were, draw down or raise the heavy protective metal gates, yet they were always up or down at the expected times. It also was odd that my friends never mentioned the place. I'm certain they would have mentioned it at some point if any of them had ever gone in, or if they had heard anything at all concerning its owners. Yes, the entire affair was curious, and a bit disturbing to me, I admit. I withdrew from the window, but not before observing a gathering of crows perched high in a ginkgo tree across the courtyard attending my building.

Margaret's reading glasses lay on the coffee table, where she had forgotten them. They had been there three days now, since Friday, and though she didn't own a second pair, she had not come 'round to collect them. Her flat was three doors down the corridor, nestled around the bend, between the corridor's fold and the compactor room for our floor. Considering this proximity, the distance and the toil for her aging bones (she often referred to herself this way) of getting here could not have been the reason of her seeming abandonment of the glasses. No. Knowing Margaret, she was probably setting her flat to sixes and sevens looking for the things. Oh Margaret, my dear Margaret, how I love you so very much.

I drew, again, near the window and observed the corner store. I looked, once more, at the courtyard and noted the empty benches there. None of my friends were yet out. As is their custom, they were probably waiting for the postman before venturing down, a sensible practice of managing one's movements in order to conserve precious human energy. *It shouldn't be long now.*

I gathered my keys and a navy blue shawl cardigan strewn over a chair, then started out. As is my habit, I scanned the room for any item I might have meant to take with me but foolishly was about to leave behind. Margaret's reading glasses seized my gaze. I let them rest, then closed the door behind me, setting the deadbolt

in place before double-twisting the cylinder beneath to
engage the second lock.

*

I perspire whenever I sit alone in the courtyard. I
know this. Although I have never understood why this
should be, it is invariably the case. I've often thought what
a tragic, if not pathetic, figure I must appear to be, sitting
here on a plank bench dabbing my brow, throat, and nape
while waiting for my friends to arrive. The doorman was
cordial when reminding me that mail is not delivered on
Sundays.

"Oh, Mrs. Manchester. You remember, don't you, that
the mailman doesn't work on Sundays? Not in the United
States. Not in New York City."

The brute. Was he condescending to me? No, I
suppose not. It was, perhaps, elder-speak—that idiotic,
childlike way some younger people speak to their elders.
Soon they'll refer to themselves in the third person, as is
the annoying habit of many first-time parents when they
discourse with their younger brand.

"Oh, Mrs. Manchester. Mr. Doorman *doesn't know*
when Mr. Repairman will fix the elevator." Ridiculous. I
suppose it *is* condescension, though well-meaning.

Three doormen regularly serve our building; one per
eight-hour shift, not including, of course, the maintenance
lad who sits in when a doorman takes his lunch. Raul, the
boy with whom I had just had the unpleasant exchange,
works the 8 a.m. to 4 p.m. shift. He is a Hispanic fellow
with bushy, connected brows, and seems to always have
a mousy look in his eye for me, one that speaks volumes

against the ruffian who I could tell dominated his earlier years. My dear Margaret is so fond of this one, though she can never pin down precisely why. I, for my part, am not too sure about him. I feel there is still something fierce in the man that would bite if the fruits of his patience were not realized.

Then there is Maurice; an Italian chap, I believe. Margaret was slow in warming to this one, citing his "inability to observe social cues" whenever she wished politely to end a conversation with him. I suggested to Margaret that he seemed a nice enough fellow and would probably observe social cues if he recognized them. The Italians, I remind her, can be a spirited lot once they get going. Maurice worked the 4 p.m. to midnight shift and was the most conversational of the boys at the desk.

"Really, Mary," she had said to me. "It just won't do for you to continue referring to these men as *boys*. If you would bother to speak to them, you would know that some of them have children of their own."

"Oh, Margaret, my dear," I had answered. "You know I mean no pernicious thing. It's just that they're so young. Besides, I would never call them that to their faces. And you quite already know my feelings regarding conversations with them. I don't believe they *want* our conversation, Margaret. They oblige us."

I placed myself on a different bench, one beneath a subtly swaying tree of a species I had never been able to identify, and fished about in my handbag for Margaret's reading glasses, purposing to give them to her if she were to sit with me. We have never sat on this bench, neither separately or together, this is true, but this bench faces the store and I was determined, this day, to solicit some remark from Margaret concerning the shop's mysterious

arrival and awkward presence in the neighborhood. I
could not find her reading glasses.

Carefully, I shifted the contents of my handbag about,
to no avail. I distinctly remembered placing them there.
Had I given them to her already? Perhaps on the way
down to the courtyard? That must have been it. What
was I saying now? Yes, something about the two doormen
who serve this building, Raul and Maurice. Yes, yes.
There is much too much work for two doormen. I have
always maintained that a third should be taken on. Let the
expense be damned.

Margaret, sitting beside me, wore a pair of black slacks
and a purple woolen sweater she once confided to me
was her favorite, it having been given to her by her late
husband just prior to his passing. To accessorize it, she
had loosely wrapped a beige cashmere scarf around her
neck that lent a particular glow to her cheeks, making her
appear as though she had recently been kissed and was still
flush. I'm always happy to see her appearing healthy this
way. It gives me hope and summons to me a sense of peace,
from somewhere I wouldn't dare go to fetch it.

She sat to my right (it was her peculiar way to always
sit to my right) and gazed at me for a long moment. Again,
today, she did not speak. Lately, she had taken to not
speaking while we sat in the courtyard. I don't know why.

"Margaret, my dear, I do believe you're fading
somewhat. Why is this so? Soon, if you continue this way,
you'll be an absolute transparency. Why is this so? What's
wrong, Margaret? Tell me, your dear friend." I paused my
speech and removed my hand from my purse. "Dear, have
I given you your glasses?"

She sat, silent, with her hands clasped in her lap. The
age spots on the back of her left hand seemed to me to

swim—no, to float—on her skin. I stared at her interlaced fingers for a time before fully comprehending the cause of the oddity. My eyes were tearing, that's what it was. That damnable tearing. This happens sometimes when I sit alone in the courtyard. And this, sitting alone, I'm sure was solely responsible for the seeming blurring and wobbling of Margaret's age spots on her hand. But I was *not* alone. Why, then, were my eyes tearing? Margaret continued her gaze on me but would not speak. Her eyes were worrisome, but my question, or the way I had asked it, provoked the ends of her mouth to bend upwards to smile.

I turned momentarily to see if any of our friends had yet ventured into the courtyard. I've learned that it was always best to spot them and beckon them to me before they sat elsewhere and got comfortable there. It's unbearable, the look they give me if I ask them to stand just after they've sat. But there was no one. No one had yet come. *It shouldn't be long now.* The remnants of a fleeting thought reminded me that the crows in the ginkgo tree seemed to grow in number with each passing day. Strangely, each day, fewer and fewer of my friends would arrive, so that I might point out this phenomenon to them. Today, so far, there was no one.

I shifted in my seat and happened to catch sight of a few browned leaves being whipped by the wind in circles on the pathway. Duped by their ferryman, they had lost their will, I thought. Their purpose, that allotment of meaning once afforded them, had been exhausted. They twirled now in a somber death dance—without feeling, without being felt; tumbling and twirling into obscurity. I noticed them, regretfully, then turned toward Margaret to forget them.

"You know, Margaret, I waited and waited for you to

come along and claim your glasses. How *ever* did you get by without reading?" I tried bringing a bit of buoyancy to my voice to assist my sinking spirit, but the result resembled desperation, so I let the effort go and continued in my usual way. "It's been a fortnight, at least. Were you very angry with me for not bringing them?"

Margaret's smile morphed into some despondent sort of thing. Her lips, now tightly pressed, displaced their natural curves. Loneliness peeped silently from her eyes. *Was* it loneliness? She leaned into me on the bench as if prepared to speak in confidence, but she said nothing. This was her way, her thing to do, to lean into you that way. You felt more intimately connected to her, and tender emotions were communicated to you by the action. It was a warming thing to do, though I doubt she realized any of this.

"Really, Margaret. You must answer me sometime. If it's about the glasses, I'm sorry. I should have brought them sooner. But I have brought them today. Won't you forgive me and speak? Margaret, my dear Margaret. And, speaking of reading glasses, why have you suddenly begun wearing them when you have nothing with you to read? You will destroy your vision, dear."

I repositioned myself so as to no longer face her but, rather, to face the store across the street. I noticed for the first time that its awning seemed tilted, as if its right side were about to fall. The decrepit thing must have hung thus for years, without a soul to fix it. Now, the crashing down of its bulk on the head of some passerby seemed imminent. I worried but said nothing to Margaret about it, or the store. I wanted her to notice them. I needed *her* to notice them first.

"You know, Margaret, I sometimes cry when I'm in my

flat alone. No one sees me, of course. No one hears me. I *do* so miss our times conversing together. It's unforgivable, Margaret: It's been a fortnight. I know I could have come to see you, but I was so sure you would come. You *always* come. I've waited and waited."

At that moment, I glanced at Margaret and noticed that she now eyed the store. *Was* it the store? It seemed so. As she regarded it, scenes from an inner tragedy played in her eyes, toggling her facial expressions between reticent fear and longing. I understood, immediately, what she was experiencing. It was apprehension, a miscarriage of faith accompanying the tug of compulsion.

"What are you looking at, Margaret, that has you so ill-at-ease? Tell me. And *please* stop straining your eyes by peering through your reading glasses."

With the exception of a quiver that I noticed vibrating the lower outline of her bottom lip, she was unchanged by my words. I looked at Margaret more intently now and was seized by the ominous remarks made by the lines of her face. My words breached the air.

"Margaret? My dear? Tell me. What's troubling you? What do you see?"

"I see a *thing*. Mary, I see it. It *sees me*. Mary, I am afraid."

She had spoken to me for the first time in so very long, it made me tremble to hear her voice.

"Afraid of what, my dear? What sees you? That store? You're all riddles and rhymes." The slowness of her speech was unsettling.

"No. It's inside, Mary. Inside. I see it moving whenever I look. Only when I look does it move."

"Margaret? You're odd today. When you're not looking, how can you know whether this *thing* is moving

94

or not?" I glanced at the store and noticed nothing different from what I had observed previously. "Come, give me your glasses. *What's* moving? Is it moving now?"

"Yes. It wants me to come. To come. Will you come with me, Mary?"

"I most certainly will not go with you into that damnable place! And if you go, Margaret, the act will force me to ring the police, forthwith." My words came fast, startling me, even though I had produced them. I was anxious for Margaret and wanted to take her with me from the courtyard to some better place—but, for us, there was no better place than the courtyard. Margaret stood and tilted her face a bit towards the sky. I knew the movements. Over time I had become familiar with their meaning. Together, they were not a posture of defiance. No. They were more a pleading with an unseen source for strength.

"Will you abandon me in this, Mary? Will you? *Abandon* me?"

Stung by her words, I struggled to stand; to bind her injurious questions with the urgency of my response. But I could not stand.

It was then the winds came, and with them a chill I thought would end me. They thrashed the trees with their tumultuous tongues and stirred dust and grass chaff high into the air. I closed my eyes and shied my lowered head from their insistence while clutching closed the collar of my cardigan. The words Margaret had spoken echoed as flatly as tapped tin in my ears.

Abandon me?

The winds calmed. I raised my head and noticed Margaret exiting the courtyard. With each step, the outline of her sweater became less distinct, her figure and gait less known to me against the backdrop of the store. I picked up her reading glasses from the seat beside me, where she had forgotten them, and stood, watching her retreating purple mark continue its float from the curbside and into the street. It was Margaret's way to *float,* as if careless, when she walked. I had told her so, in admiration, many times before. My legs trembled when she entered the place. When I looked through the dirty shop windows for a glimpse of her, I noticed a large shadow move toward the door.

Oh Margaret, my dear Margaret. I sometimes cry when I am alone in my flat. No one sees me, of course. No one hears me. It is *you* who have abandoned *me* this day.

I placed Margaret's reading glasses in my handbag and entered the pathway leading to the building. My friends would not join me today, that much was clear. Perhaps was it the wind that dissuaded them? Pity. I did *so* look forward to continuing my chat with the new resident who had moved in last week. Maurice, I believe is what he said his name was. I don't believe Margaret has ever met him. I did *so* much want to share with him my observation of the daily amassing of crows atop the ginkgo tree; to hear his exclamations and repeated reservations about the store and its degenerated state, when I would finally point it out to him. I did. In truth, I did.

I entered the building and gave Raul, the doorman, a stern eye, to which he responded by looking askance. Did I mention him? A rough sort of fellow he is, beneath all that self-applied polish. I could always tell such things. It's the hands, you see. The hands are a logbook of a life. When one polishes oneself in life, the polish gets into the hands and gives them a dull, laborer's look. Conversely, when one is polished by society, the hands remain clean and inviting,

showing themselves to the world as free from life's millions
of miserable encumbrances. I addressed Raul directly.

"Tell me, Raul, has the postman come?"

"The *mailman*, Mrs. Manchester?"

"Yes, the postman. Has he come?"

The man looked and picked at the undersides of his
fingernails while he spoke. I thought him a thoroughbred
knave for doing it.

"Mrs. Manchester, you remember, don't you, that the
mailman doesn't work on Sundays? Not in the United
States. Not in New York City."

"Very well, then. Fine. But you will ring me the
moment he arrives? The very moment?"

"Yes, Mrs. Manchester. I can do that for you." He
rubbed his thick brows with his left index finger and
thumb, all the while looking at the countertop before him.
I continued my steps to the elevator to escape the insolence.

Margaret, my dear. Is it too late to come? Is it?

*

I closed the door behind me and twisted the latch,
noting how the clunk of the deadbolt as it engaged
the door's metal frame seemed synonymous with the
despondency setting in my heart. After resting my
handbag and shawl on the chair, I glanced about me and
caught sight of Margaret's reading glasses on the coffee
table, where I had left them. They commanded my gaze
for a time, and soon after, their presence there brought on
a debilitating confusion. Was it only a moment it lasted?
Perhaps. Perhaps not. For a while I scarcely recognized
my flat. Then it passed; the confusion passed, and with

clarity of mind I entered my bedroom to pack an overnight bag. Yes, I *would* join Margaret.

While I assembled my garments, the winds returned and beat against my living room windows as though attempting to alert me of a consequential change outside. I resisted the urge to draw near the panes to visually interrogate their outdoors. I chose, instead, to focus on my packing while remaining fully aware that my packing probably was pointless. After all, Margaret had gone into the store and was received there, while having nothing more than the clothing on her frame. I witnessed this. But determined to join Margaret *there*, I packed nonetheless. Wherever *there* was did not matter. It had to be better than here. It *had* to be better than the courtyard. Certainly, Margaret thought so.

*

A clinking crash of glass sounded from the living room, giving me a fright. The caw that followed nearly paralyzed me. For a time I stood by my bed, beside the opened travel bag, unable to compose myself sufficiently to place into it the black satin slip I had folded. I listened as the fractured silence revealed a tapping. Its irregular regularity entranced me. In time, when the draft resuscitated my mind, I placed my slip into the bag and moved to the living room's entranceway.

It stood there, on the coffee table, positioning and cocking its head in various positions while examining Margaret's reading glasses. In areas, its lustrous black feathers, with their shimmering purple sheen, reflected the white light of the outdoors, leaving me with the impression that the thing had pinched off a bit of sky to adorn itself. I loved it instantly, and I watched as it stepped carefully about on the coffee table, avoiding the shards of broken window lying there. Its claws against the inlaid glass of the table were what produced the tapping. It didn't seem to notice me. Instead, it seemed preoccupied with the reading glasses near it.

It was a large black bird, quite possibly one of the many I had noticed atop the ginkgo tree at the furthermost corner of the courtyard. A crow? *Was* it a crow? I regarded it a while, surprised that it wasn't hurt in the collision with the window, but I became tentative as it persisted in familiarizing itself with Margaret's glasses. Unsure why, I felt I *knew* the creature, as though its soul had once touched mine in some intimate way. Perhaps there was something about the way it moved, the way it leaned into a thing while examining it. Yes, perhaps. My affinity for the creature notwithstanding, I remained still and did not attempt to go near it. I didn't dare move.

It was with a sense of despair and a feeling of claustrophobia that I watched as the black bird took Margaret's reading glasses in its beak and flew through the window to rejoin the outside world. I traced its flight with my gaze as best I could. I thought I saw the thing perch with the other crows in the tree across the courtyard, but a moment later, I could not be sure. It was with this hope, however, that I stood by the broken window a long while, praying that a glimmer of light would reflect from Margaret's reading glasses, but there was nothing. Nothing but the murder of crows.

I lowered my gaze to the courtyard and accepted that none of my friends would venture out this day. Was Margaret the last one? Was *I* all who was left?

99

The store was gone. Its dirty windows and soiled cloth canopy had somehow been removed. I swallowed when registering the absence. In the store's place was an awning-less fruit and vegetable shop that appeared well frequented; its wooden outdoor carts displayed colorful rows of oranges, plums, apples, and other items that tempted the neighborhood souls to draw near them as a cool spring does parched tongues. I wanted to die.

Tired. Tired of the chilled breeze against my face, I turned toward my bedroom. *Tired.* Tired of the cheerless, overcast sky and accursed courtyard, I turned toward my bedroom. There was nothing else. There was nothing more. All there was, was nothing.

It's true. I sometimes cry when I am in my flat alone. No one sees me, of course. No one hears me.

Tired. I sat off the side of my bed, beside my open travel bag. *Tired.* Yes, but there was, in fact, *something*, wasn't there? I remember it. In my handbag, where I had forgotten them, there *were* Margaret's reading glasses. I remember it. *That* was something. Yes. In my handbag there were Margaret's reading glasses. *That* was not nothing.

A Note About the Author

IIMANI DAVID was born in Brooklyn, New York. An avid and successful experimenalist of the literary impressionist style, he debuted in *Anathema Rhodes: Dreams* the literary techniques "maypoling" and "vertical storytelling" to enhance the surreal sense of his characters' mental and emotional experiences.

In *The Bastard* David pioneered a literary technique called "echoing". Also referred to as "shadowing", this technique is defined as the mimicking of dialogue by characters after a shifted context or place in time.

In *Pathétique* David experiments with his created technique, "staccato". Named after its musical articulation, staccato uses a rapid succession of short sentences to move the reader quickly along the same psychological vein as the character.

We encourage readers to contact the author with questions and comments concerning this title:

i@iimanidavid.com
www.iimanidavid.com

Concerning the Type

This book was set in Granjon, a type designed by George W. Jones (born 1860 in Upton-on-Severn, died 1942 in Worcestershire) for the English branch of Linotype in 1928. Jones used a type cut by Claude Garamond as his model, but because several other Garamonds were on the market in the 1920's, he decided to name his Granjon.

Jones' Granjon more closely matches Garamond's type than many modern faces bearing the name. Numerous Garamond revivals of the 1920's were later shown to be actually based on the types of Jean Jannon.